Ron Ellis was studying for a degree in librarianship at Liverpool Polytechnic when he became involved in the sixties Merseybeat phenomenon. He managed several beat groups in the city, sold records to The Beatles and became the North West's first mobile D.J.

In the seventies he was appointed Northern Promotions Manager for Warner Brothers Records, escorted Miss World and various pop stars on UK tours and made his own self penned record, *Boys on the Dole*, which reached No. 7 in the New Wave charts in 1979.

Since then, he has worked as a salesman, actor, librarian, journalist, lecturer in Creative Writing, photographer, landlord, teashop proprietor and broadcaster.

Ron stills lives on Merseyside with his wife and two daughters. In between writing crime novels he is studying for a PhD in Music at the University of Liverpool. He is the football correspondent for the *Southport Champion*, has a regular show on local radio, appears in Yorkshire TV's nightly weather forecast advert and owns a property company in London's Dockland near the Millennium Dome.

PLAYGROUND PETS

When elderly opera 'queen' Max Cadamarteri is found dead in bed with his throat cut open, Detective Chief Inspector Glass is called in to investigate. Glass also has the Police Christmas Party to attend to, which turns out to be a disaster when a blue movie is shown and Detective Sergeant Evans recognises his under-age goddaughter in the cast. The search is now on for the peddlars of porn. Meanwhile, Glass's son-in-law, Detective Chief Inspector Robin Knox, is on the trail of a serial murderer after a number of young girls have been found dead and identically mutilated.

Books by Ron Ellis
Published by The House of Ulverscroft:

MURDER FIRST CLASS
THE SNORT OF KINGS
JOURNAL OF A COFFIN DODGER

RON ELLIS

PLAYGROUND PETS

A Detective Chief Inspector Glass Mystery

Complete and Unabridged

ULVERSCROFT
Leicester

First Large Print Edition
published 2001

British Library CIP Data

Ellis, Ron, *1941 –*
    Playground pets.—Large print ed.—
Ulverscroft large print series: mystery
1. Detective and mystery stories
2. Large type books
I. Title
823.9'14 [F]

ISBN 0–7089–4357–8

Published by
F. A. Thorpe (Publishing)
Anstey, Leicestershire
Set by Words & Graphics Ltd.
Anstey, Leicestershire
Printed and bound in Great Britain by
T. J. International Ltd., Padstow, Cornwall

This book is printed on acid-free paper

1

'I don't know why we didn't stick with *Cinderella*.' Max Cadamarteri emerged from the back legs of a pantomime cow, sweat running down his cheeks in rivulets, his flabby stomach hanging over a pair of greying Wolsey cotton trunks.

'Because we did it last year, that's why, and the year before,' returned a voice from the front portion of the farmyard creature. 'So this year, we went for *Jack and the Beanstalk* for a change.'

'At least there wasn't a cow in *Cinderella*,' puffed Max. 'The Ugly Sisters were a doddle compared to this. I'm sixty-two. I'm getting too old for crouching around for two hours at a time.' He pushed the thinning strands of long grey hair out of his eyes. 'Roll on the summer.'

'You can say that again.' His elderly companion disengaged himself from the front of the huge fur wrapping and emerged into the backstage area of the theatre. 'Give me *Don Giovanni* anytime.' He led the way to their dressing room, his tall, stooping figure looking incongruous in Aertex vest and briefs.

'The pity is, Gregory, *Don Giovanni* doesn't pay the bills and Jack and the Sodding Beanstalk does. And we do like an opulent lifestyle, don't we love? The odd weeks of Mozart and Puccinni, fun though it may be, won't keep us in the flat in Chelsea.'

'Not to mention the vino.'

'Great show there, chaps. Well done.' The tall familiar figure of one of Britain's best loved comedians, resplendent in his Alice the Cook pantomime dame costume, overtook them down the corridor.

The two halves of the pantomime cow nodded a greeting.

'By the way, Max, you were going to let me have that tip for the King George on Boxing Day. Don't forget, will you.'

'That's right, I was. Suny Bay, Harry. That'll be the winner. You can still get a good price.'

'Write it down for me will you, there's a good chap. I've got an awful memory.' He followed them to their dressing room and waited whilst Max found a biro and wrote the horse's name on a scrap of paper. He handed it to the comedian.

'Thanks a lot. I'll cut you in on the champagne if it wins. Good audience for a Monday, eh?'

'Patronising git,' murmured Gregory shutting the door when he'd gone. 'I'm sure he's having it off with wotzername, you know, the girl who's playing Jack.'

'Marsha, Marsha Flint.'

'Young enough to be his granddaughter.'

Max slumped onto a wooden chair in the corner of their dressing room that was more like a tiny cell. The only lighting was a bare hundred-watt bulb and a wide ledge ran alongside a mirrored back wall on the end of which was fixed a small washbasin.

'You know, I don't think I can manage another season of this.' He was still panting from the evening's exertions.

'You say that every year.'

'This time I mean it. I promise you, Gregory, this will be my last pantomime.'

Little did Max Cadamarteri know it but, not only was Jack and the Beanstalk to be his last pantomime, this was his last ever performance.

★ ★ ★

The following lunchtime, Gregory Oliver returned from a trip to the supermarket to find the body of his friend lying on their magnificent king size bed with his throat cut open.

Detective Chief Inspector Glass surveyed the scene of the crime not an hour later. A large man in his fifties, he wore a brown greatcoat and a battered trilby that wouldn't have made the shelves at Oxfam.

The actors lived on the second floor of a block of six modern flats. The patrol car that had been summoned by Gregory's 999 call had alerted the Scotland Yard officers once the nature of the crime had been ascertained.

The uniformed constable outlined the scenario to Glass. 'They were playing in pantomime in Richmond, Jack and the Beanstalk.'

'Lived here together did they?' The inspector looked meaningfully at the double bed, the black silk sheets stained with blood from the body, which lay on them.

'I believe so.'

'A couple of shirtlifters then?' murmured Glass, glancing round the pink and gilt bedroom. Gregory was being given medicinal brandy in the lounge.

'I don't think we're allowed to say that anymore, sir,' ventured his companion, Sergeant Moon, who was a good twenty years his junior.

Glass ignored him. 'Crime of passion, perhaps? His lover finds he's been two-timed, slits his partner's throat in a jealous rage then rings us to clean up the mess.'

Moon looked doubtful. 'A bit too simple, wouldn't you say? He was the one who rang the ambulance.'

'You should know by now, Sergeant, that the two people most likely to have committed any murder are the person who finds the body and the deceased's spouse. And in this case they're one and the same and queer to boot. What more do you want?'

'Hardly conclusive, though, sir.'

Glass merely grunted. 'Forensic should be here any day. We might as well leave them to it. Let's go and talk to the old queen, I mean,' he corrected himself, catching Moon's glance, 'the bereaved.'

Gregory sat by the window, being comforted by a uniformed constable. He looked even older than his sixty-five years.

'Max and I have been together since 1952, Chief Inspector,' he replied in answer to the detective's question. 'We met in Vienna on the opera circuit.'

'You're both singers then?'

'Good Lord, yes.'

'So what are you doing buried inside a stuffed farm animal in a provincial pantomime?'

Gregory looked embarrassed. 'We do pantomime at Christmas because it's regular income and it pays well.'

'What about the rest of the year?'

'We latch onto some touring Opera company, or get a season somewhere. Sometimes it has to be Gilbert & Sullivan or, if we're really desperate, operetta. I mean, I love Ivor but *King's Rhapsody* isn't *Aida* is it?'

Glass, whose musical appreciation was limited to Chas and Dave and The Beverley Sisters, shook his head in agreement.

'Mind you, nowadays, nobody wants the full operas anymore. They ask for excerpts and highlights. I blame CD's and all those Greatest Hits collections. We've more chance of a 'Three Tenors' tour or a 'Night at the Opera' than the real thing. Do you know, we've only had one proper show all summer, a week in Scarborough with *Figaro*. And now this.'

'Isn't it a bit early for the pantomime season? I thought they only started on Boxing Day. It's still nearly a fortnight to Christmas.'

'Bums on seats, that's what it's all about. Some of the kids have broken up already so to hang with tradition. It's no different than buying strawberries in November or Hot Cross Buns in July. No respect for the seasons anymore. Sadly, we live in a profit-led culture.'

'I know what you mean,' agreed Glass. 'When I was a lad, you played cricket in the summer and the football never kicked off until the end of August.'

'Things aren't what they used to be, Chief Inspector.'

'My sentiments entirely.' The policeman could have written a book on the subject and was pleased to find someone who shared his point of view. He was even prepared to believe Gregory Oliver might not, after all, be a vicious killer.

'So we have pantomime at the beginning of December. This is our second week.'

'And how has it been going?' asked Glass. 'More to the point, what has happened at the theatre that could have led to the tragic murder of your, er, companion.'

At the mention of Max, Gregory burst into tears again. 'Nothing at all,' he said. 'We get on well with everyone in the show. Max hadn't an enemy in the world. He was a lovely man.'

'Who's in this pantomime?'

'Harry Hooper.'

'The comedian?'

'There's only one Harry Hooper. 'The loveable Cockney comic', or so it says in the programme.'

'You don't agree?'

'I've seen his night-club act. Makes Chubby Brown look like Sooty. I've no time for filth, Chief Inspector. Not on the public stage. Demeans our profession. It ought to be banned.'

'And who else is in the cast?' Glass had no desire to get into a debate about censorship.

'Marsha Flint. She plays Jack. I believe she came to us from an Australian soap series.'

'She's had a couple of hit records,' interposed Sergeant Moon. 'She's only eighteen.'

'Too young for him,' muttered Gregory.

'What?' barked Glass.

'Hooper. They say he's been having his evil way with her.'

'Really? I suppose that's not surprising when you think about it.' Harry Hooper's private life was a constant source of material for the tabloids. His succession of progressively younger wives, even younger mistresses, barroom fights and battles with the bottle had enthralled readers for years. Yet still he retained the image of a loveable Cockney rogue, to which age had merely added an almost avuncular facade. 'Do you think it was true?'

'Probably. He's the sort of man who'd have a snake if it stopped sliding long enough.'

'Mmmm.' Glass thought it was a shame it

wasn't Harry Hooper's body they had found. There would probably have been a lot more suspects to work on. Instead, he had to make do with this popular bit player with not an enemy in the world.

'So you know of nobody in the cast who could have had the slightest reason to kill Mr. Cadamarteri?'

Gregory emitted a long sigh. 'Nobody at all. We got on well with everyone. On a superficial level, of course. None of us were close friends, we'd not known each other long enough, but there was certainly no one who had any quarrel with Max or I.'

'No professional jealousy?'

'Not really. We're all in different fields. Mind you, we do have a spot just before the end when we all come out of costume and sing a selection from our normal repertoires.'

'Oh yes?'

'Yes. Marsha Flint performs her hits that the sergeant mentioned earlier. She uses these frightfully loud backing tapes, shatter your hearing aid at fifty yards, but the audience seems to like it. Then, of course, Harry Hooper has had some success in what I believe they call the easy listening market, like Ken Dodd and Max Bygraves before him.'

Glass shivered. 'I've heard him.'

'More musak than music,' commented Gregory wickedly. 'He gets the band to play louder and the audience to sing along to hide his vocal deficiencies.'

Nobody can slip in a bitchy aside like a woofter, thought Glass, who had himself regarded Harry Hooper as a poor man's Des O'Connor.

'And Maxie and I would do a couple of humorous numbers, *Mad dogs and Englishmen* and *Don't put your daughter on the stage Mrs. Worthington*. All played for laughs of course. Opera would be too much for a pantomime audience.'

'Nothing to incur the resentment of the others then?'

'Unless Hooper had a secret yearning to be Noel Coward, no.'

The Chief Inspector tried another tack. 'Who is likely to benefit from your friend's death?'

'You mean who will he have left his money to? The answer is I, although, I can tell you, he had precious little to leave. Max and I didn't believe in saving. We enjoyed life to the full. But I'd give every penny I ever earned to have dear Maxie back with me again.' Gregory burst into uncontrollable tears.

Glass was not known for his excessive

sentimentality and he ignored the histrionics. 'Somebody obviously had a grievance against him. Had he any other enemies? Did he owe money to someone?'

Gregory shook his head to both suggestions and blew his nose into a large silk handkerchief.

'It wasn't a burglary,' Sergeant Moon offered, helpfully. 'Nothing appears to be missing or even disturbed. Whoever it was broke in, slashed the victim's throat whilst he slept and left as quickly as he came. The front door lock was a simple one, easily forced.'

'An admirable summing up,' grated Glass. 'All we need is the name of this mystery visitor and we can all go home. I take it you can't supply that as well?'

Moon admitted he couldn't. 'None of the neighbours appear to be in,' he said. 'The uniform men have been round the other flats.'

'They'll be at work, it's Tuesday morning.'

'I don't think so, sir. These are retirement flats.'

'These two weren't retired.'

'They qualify though. They're over 55.'

The inspector ignored the last remark. 'We can't do much until we know the time of death and the weapon used.' He turned to the bereft actor. 'The pathologist and the forensic people will be here shortly,' he informed him. 'I've no more questions for the time being.' He tried to sound kindly but he made it seem like a threat. 'We'll be in touch, Mr. Oliver.'

Gregory bit his lip. 'I should have been at the matinee now. This is the first performance I've missed for twenty years.'

'Understandable in the circumstances,' sympathised Glass. 'They couldn't have a two legged cow.' He consulted his watch. It was four o'clock. 'Sergeant, I want you to get down to the theatre and interview all the cast and the backstage crew. In fact,' he added as an afterthought, 'you might as well speak to the front of house people and management as well. Somebody must know something. And you'd better hurry, before the evening performance gets underway.'

'Where shall you be, sir?'

'Me?' snapped Glass. 'I shall be at a party. In case you hadn't noticed, Moon, we are entering the festive season.'

2

Stella the Striptease Dancer put her tongue between her lips coquettishly and pointed her naked breasts at the audience. She would have preferred to swing them but, unfortunately, they were not large enough for this. Instead, she shook her body from side to side in the forlorn hope that the movement might produce at least a compensatory wobble.

Her predecessor on the stage of the Compton Road Welfare and Social Club had not had this problem. At the climax of her act, urged on by the enthusiastic cheers of the crowd, she had forcefully compressed her elephantine bust into a silk top hat which, by virtue of the pressure from within, had remained suspended on her chest as she held both arms in the air for applause.

A man on the front row winked at Stella, a gesture that she interpreted as an invitation for a spot of naughty after the show. She winked back.

The man was a policeman.

He turned to whisper a few ribald words to his companion who responded with a laugh

13

like a gurgling drain.

This man was a policeman too.

In fact, all the men at the Compton Road Welfare and Social Club this evening were policemen. Detective Chief Inspector Glass had arranged the venue for the Annual Christmas Party, promising the club the bar profits in exchange for the free hire of the room.

The club was only too happy to oblige, as they knew from past experience that members of the police force could outdrink the Marines.

Stella the Striptease Dancer was replaced by Lem Stone, billed as The South's Greatest Comedian, a title which said little for the sense of humour of people living on the Channel side of Watford.

Mr. Stone, a daytime Social Security recipient, had spent the early part of the evening at the bar with the punters and was now as intoxicated as most of them. His little trip as he reached falteringly for the microphone stand and fell flat on his face brought the biggest cheer of the evening.

Meanwhile, in the dressing room, amidst the cleaning materials, empty beer barrels and spare toilet rolls, two barmen were straining to prise the silk top hat from the bust of the first exotic dancer with the aid of a screwdriver, a dessert spoon and a bar of wet soap.

Lem Stone's act went down well, which reflected little credit on the cultural proclivities of the audience, concentrating as it did on racial inequality, constipation, the human reproductive organs and the sexual habits of the clergy.

It reminded Glass of Gregory Oliver's comments about Harry Hooper. At least Hooper was good looking, he thought, whilst Lem Stone resembled a computerised reconstruction of the recently excavated Neanderthal skull referred to in the tabloids as Mr. Bogman.

Stone's monologue was sprinkled liberally with fashionable swear words and delivered in a peculiar nasal whine, reminiscent of a lawnmower being pulled across a gravel path.

'A bit different from the usual nights, eh Mr. Glass?' The white-jacketed barman refilled the detective's glass with Southern Comfort.

'I'll say, Granville.' Only two nights previously, Glass had been dancing a slow foxtrot with his widowed friend Mrs. Lewthwaite in front of the very stage where The South's Greatest Comedian now performed.

'They can't half get through some ale, your

lot, I'll give them that.'

'What!' exclaimed Glass. 'The club should be able to buy a new billiard table out of tonight's little shindig.' He drank a little faster as his own contribution. 'If not a couple. Hang on, here they come.'

The lights went up to signal the end of Lem Stone's spot and an oily-haired compere came onstage to announce that, after a fifteen-minute interval, there would be a film show. Most of his words were lost as the audience stampeded to the bar like a herd of crazed bison.

'Some bonny lasses you've got us tonight, Walter,' shouted Detective Inspector Washington who hailed from Whitley Bay. 'I would'na mind a few minutes with them after the show.'

A cackle of raucous laughter from his fellow officers as they jostled for service suggested he would not be alone in his fantasy.

'What's on next?' asked a fledgling constable.

Two men were erecting a large screen television and video recorder on to the stage.

'A couple of films, I believe. Confiscated by the Porn Squad in Soho last week.'

'Can't be bad.'

'Oh, I don't know. Seen one, you've seen 'em all. I prefer a live show myself.' This from Detective Sergeant Snape who had spent sixteen years in The Porn Squad and liked to give the impression that he regularly attended erotic events usually witnessed only by Arab oil sheikhs and reporters from the popular Sunday press.

'*Playground Pets* one of them is called.' A keen observer was inspecting the video cassette box. Glass shuddered. He preferred his women to be of menopausal age.

'Here we are, the lights are going down.' There was a dash for the chairs and attention was focussed on the screen as the title *Convent Capers* came into view.

The opening sequence of the film showed two nuns walking side by side along a busy street. They turned into an apartment building and the camera zoomed close in as they entered the lift in time to catch the first nun pull up her habit to reveal black suspenders with matching pubic hair, a revelation greeted by offensive suggestions from the more inebriate of the officers present.

During the ascension of the lift, the second nun assumed a kneeling position commensurate with her calling and proceeded to administer oral stimulation to her Holy Sister, a diversion they enjoyed right up to the fifth floor.

There, a happy surprise awaited them.

A large black man was waiting outside the elevator gates. He conducted the two nuns into a sparsely furnished flat whereupon he wilfully, openly, lewdly and obscenely exposed himself to them contrary to Section 4 of the 1824 Vagrancy Act.

The watching arm of the Law shouted their encouragement, urging the black man to 'get on with it' and 'give them one'. He didn't disappoint them, mounting the first nun with rising enthusiasm whilst the other speedily divested herself of her robes in preparation for her turn.

For the next nineteen minutes, they performed a variety of couplings until the black man collapsed apparently with exhaustion, in the final frame.

Loud and appreciative applause greeted the credits and a ten-minute interval followed to allow everyone to replenish their glasses yet again.

It was in an atmosphere of lustful anticipation that they resumed their seats for the second film, the promised *Playground Pets*.

This opened with a middle-aged man wearing a long raincoat standing beside a park where a group of three teenage girls were playing on the swings. The man obligingly turned towards the camera and opened his raincoat to afford the audience a preliminary inspection of his credentials.

'What a whopper,' roared an overweight traffic controller who was replete with Lambs Navy Rum.

The celluloid hero, who bore some resemblance to Charles Laughton in his role as Quasimodo, walked over to the swings and took from his pocket three lollipops that he handed in turn to the teenagers.

The camera cut to a bedroom. The man, still in his raincoat, had the three girls lined up against the wall. They all looked under age and apprehensive.

The mood in the audience dramatically changed. Nobody laughed. Nobody shouted out. They all watched the screen intently.

The man held out a five-pound note to the tallest girl who slowly took off her dress. She wore nothing underneath. She looked frightened. The man ran his fingers over her unformed bosom. Slowly, he opened his raincoat and moved menacingly forward but he never reached her.

'Stop the film,' bellowed the stentorian voice of Detective Sergeant Evans. 'That child is my goddaughter.'

★ ★ ★

Linzi Pennington looked barely thirteen in her school uniform. In the evening, with the judicious application of make up and an uplift bra, she had no difficulty in purchasing a bottle of Two Dogs at any pub or club in town.

In reality, Linzi was fifteen years old and, despite her evening appearance, not at all streetwise.

She had met Gordon Nightingale at a local discotheque. Girls were admitted free of charge before 9.30 p.m. and a complimentary ticket was easy to come by. Linzi got hers from a stack at a high street record shop.

'Do you wanna dance?' She was queuing at the bar. Her friend, Clover, had gone to the loo. She would be one up on her when she got back although the lad did look very old. At least twenty. Probably, she told herself, his fuzzy beard made him look older. Certainly, it made him attractively sinister.

In reality, Gordon Nightingale was twenty-four.

They danced, he bought her a drink and when Clover returned, he bought her one too. He was alone, there was no friend for Clover, so he danced with the two of them and entertained them with bright, inconsequential chatter until it was time for them to catch the last bus home. Whereupon he offered them a lift.

Linzi was unsure of the wisdom of accepting but Clover was with her so it seemed all right.

They dropped Clover off first.

'I'll get out here, too,' said Linzi quickly. 'I only live round the corner.'

'No trouble,' he said, with a reassuring smile. 'You'll be quite safe.' And she was. He kissed her in a manner so perfunctory that she feared he found her undesirable. So she arranged to meet him the next night to find out.

By the seventh week of their acquaintance, she allowed him to deprive her of her virginity. She thought he was rather wonderful.

One Sunday, he took her to the seaside for the day and, during the afternoon on the beach, he told her how beautiful she looked in her bikini. So beautiful, he took photographs of her in it.

Later that night, in his flat in Finchley, he took photographs of her without it. She was not too happy about this but he suggested that she took photographs of himself similarly unclothed and that, somehow, made it seem less terrible.

Then he explained about the self-timer function on the camera and how they could take photographs of the two of them together.

Doing it.

They laughed about the photographs when he brought them round a few days later. Then he told her he could sell them for £100 on the Continent where nobody knew her. £100 was a fortune. Linzi thought of the clothes she could buy with that sort of money and she agreed to let him sell them.

On her fifteenth birthday, he bought her a brooch, not too expensive in case her parents became suspicious. They knew she had a boyfriend but thought it was someone from the local youth club.

He also gave her £40 in cash. He'd taken more photographs and business was good.

'I could get £250 if we were to make a video of us making love together,' he suggested one night.

She thought. 'But the cameraman would see us doing it.'

'He wouldn't be interested, sweetheart. Those sort of men are professionals. They've seen it all before.'

By now, she was so much in love with him that if he'd asked her to do it with the cameraman as well, she would have done.

He did.

The cameraman was older than her father. He had gnarled hands and a wrinkled face that reminded her of The Hunchback of Notre Dame.

'Must I?' she asked.

He held her tightly. 'You do love me, don't you?' He sounded anxious, as if he really cared. 'You won't be on your own. There are a couple of other girls and I'll be there.'

Holding the camcorder.

The other girls were Linzi's age. They looked as nervous as she felt. She nodded to them as she reluctantly removed her clothes and allowed the revolting cameraman to abuse her young body for the future titillation of foreign audiences in such distant places as Amsterdam, Paris, Copenhagen and . . . The Compton Road Welfare and Social Club.

3

'I'll go to see her,' said Detective Chief Inspector Glass. 'You're too close to the case.' They were back at Scotland Yard. It was the day after the party.

'She is my goddaughter,' protested Sergeant Evans.

'Precisely. You're too emotionally involved which is why I'm handling it, and that is an order, Sergeant.'

'I thought you were dealing with this dead actor chap.'

'I am. Amongst a dozen other cases. Sergeant Moon was at the theatre last night asking questions.'

'Fifteen,' reflected Evans, sadly. 'God knows what her parents will say. They've lived next door to us for nearly twenty years. I knew her when she was this high.' He held out his hand as if testing for rain.

'Well you would,' said Glass unkindly. 'She being your goddaughter. You'd have been there at the baptism.'

Evans shook his head in disbelief. 'She's an only child. It'll kill her parents.'

'Better we know now,' continued Glass,

'before she ends up on the game or worse.' Evans knew that by 'worse' he meant drugs. 'She's still living at home, I take it?'

'At fifteen?'

'It has been known.'

'Yes she's at home. But you won't find anyone in till tonight. Both her parents work. Neville Pennington is a librarian and Eunice is something to do with charity. And Linzi will be at school, of course.'

'If she's not at the film studios,' commented Glass sardonically. He saw the look on Evans' face. 'Don't worry, I was only joking. I'll go after tea and I'll be tactful.'

Glass met up with Sergeant Moon in the station canteen at lunchtime. 'Any joy at the theatre?' he asked.

'Not so far.' The younger man looked weary. 'I was there until after one,' he said, 'and spoke to just about everyone but I've not found anybody with a motive. The two old boys seemed to be popular with everyone.'

'What have forensic come up with?'

'Cadamarteri was killed about ten o'clock in the morning, while Gregory Oliver was in the supermarket.'

'How about alibis for the others?'

'Most of them were in bed yesterday morning.'

25

'Let's hope they all had partners with them to confirm it.' Glass grimaced. 'Of one description or another.'

'What do you want me to do now, sir?'

'You could check Cadimateri's financial situation. See if Oliver's telling the truth. Any news of the weapon?'

'A sharp knife of some description, possibly a carving knife. Nothing found as yet. The flat's clean. I've got a team of uniformed men searching the area round the building.'

'How about a stage prop?'

Moon looked doubtful. 'I suppose it's possible.'

'Check it out. And speak to any of the cast you've not yet seen. I'm off to see Sergeant Evans' goddaughter.'

In accordance with police regulations when dealing with under age females, Glass was obliged to take along a woman police officer.

WPC Wendy Ngoomba had joined the force two years ago and had so impressed her superiors, she was speedily transferred to CID. Detective Chief Inspector Glass being, as he often liked to boast, of the 'old school', was less enthusiastic.

'In my day,' he was heard to say, 'you had to be over six feet tall to join the force and women were there to staff the canteens and clean the lavatories. Now any four-eyed, female midget can get in.'

He didn't mention Miss Ngoomba's skin, which was ebony in keeping with her Afro-Caribbean origins, but it was generally held that Glass would expect all his fellow officers to be of undiluted Anglo Saxon blood.

Wendy Ngoomba, if she was aware of these opinions, didn't mention them and chatted pleasantly to the inspector about the weather as they set off on their journey.

They presented themselves at the Pennington home as the family were finishing their evening meal. Mrs. Pennington conducted them to the dining room and insisted on them taking tea. She was small and birdlike with blue-rinsed hair, a Berkshire accent and thin, heavily ringed fingers.

Glass was placed on a chintz-covered chaise longue that blended well with the high quality antiques that filled the room. WPC Ngoomba sat on a matching armchair across the room.

'You work with Trevor Evans, I believe, Chief Inspector. I've heard him mention your name from time to time. How many sugars was it?' She juggled a floral china teapot with a matching cup and saucer.

'Three, please,' said WPC Ngoomba who had the build of a stick insect.

'None for me, thank you.' Glass remembered his diet.

'How wise. I wish I could get Neville to give it up. The white killer they call it. You should see him without his trousers on. His stomach just rolls out doesn't it, petal?'

'Petal' lowered the Financial Times from his face and grunted, causing the said stomach to swell grotesquely over the waistband of his cavalry twill slacks.

'If you don't need me, I'll repair to the study. I have some book reviews to write.' He shuffled out of the room, paper under his arm. Glass was relieved to have the mother on her own.

'It's his job, you see. Librarians spend all their time sitting down, very bad for their posture. Cake, Chief Inspector?' A creation in chocolate icing and marzipan was pushed forward. Glass shook his head and took advantage of his host's rare pause for breath to interject a question of his own.

'I've come about your daughter, Mrs. Pennington. Linzi. Are you aware of any boyfriends she might have?'

'I believe she has a young man, yes. They go to the same youth club.'

'But you haven't met him?'

'Er, no.' She caught Glass's glance of disapproval. 'But he must be all right. It's

28

a church youth club.'

'You know definitely he goes to this youth club, do you?'

For the first time, Mrs. Pennington looked worried as if she suddenly realised a Scotland Yard Inspector would hardly be calling to enquire about her daughter's progress at the ballet class.

'What do you mean? Linzi isn't in any trouble is she?'

'I think you better look at this.' From his pocket, Glass produced one of the more innocuous productions of the Linzi Pennington picture gallery and handed it to her alarmed mother.

'Oh my God! Where did you get this?' The picture showed the fifteen-year-old in a bedroom, naked. It had been extracted from the video.

'We're anxious to trace the people who took this photograph, Mrs. Pennington.' He thought it prudent not to mention moving pictures at this stage. 'We'd like to speak to Linzi when she comes home, if we may.' His tone didn't leave room for any suggestion of refusal.

'Yes, of course, but we're not expecting her till late. She's gone straight from school to the cinema with her friend Clover. But this photo, where? How?' She started to shake.

'Maybe we can call back later, then, say about eleven?'

'I suppose so.'

'Oh, and Mrs. Pennington, if she does come home early, we'd rather you didn't say anything about this to Linzi before we speak to her.'

'If you say so. Oh dear.'

'I'm not sure it's a good idea leaving her,' said WPC Ngoomba, as they returned to their car.

'Neither am I,' said Glass, 'but we'll get back there for ten thirty to make sure we don't miss her.'

But Linzi Pennington was not at the cinema. She was out with her boyfriend, Gordon. They were celebrating the £250 he'd told her he'd received for their latest video. In reality, he'd made twice that amount but he felt no reason to burden her with this information.

They sat in a dark corner of a pub off Goldhawk Road.

Having handed her her £125 'half share' of the royalties, as he quaintly liked to call them, Gordon suggested a follow up production.

'I'm not sure,' she stammered. The memories of the repulsive cameraman mauling her body had been causing her some

30

disquiet. She'd started having nightmares. She wasn't sure whether they were caused by her conscience at the immorality of her conduct, her parents had always taught her that sex outside marriage was an act of the Devil, or the thought of the elderly partner she'd been forced to accommodate.

Despite the avalanche of sexual information forced upon pre-pubescent girls by the editors of teenage magazines, Linzi was not as sophisticated as many of her age group, most of whom could have taught Masters and Johnson a thing or two.

Her activities with Gordon worried her and there was nobody with whom she could discuss her problems. Clover would have been horrified had she known what her friend was doing and to confide in her parents was unthinkable.

Gordon made everything seem perfectly normal when she was with him. Almost fun. But afterwards, on her own, the doubts began. The trouble was, she could see no way out of her dilemma. It was easier to go along with him, whatever awful new idea he suggested, rather than make a fuss.

There was always the money, she told herself, as if that would compensate for her distress.

The alternative, she didn't care to contemplate.

On two or three occasions, when she had dared venture the possibility that she wasn't happy with the situation, Gordon had made veiled threats about what would happen to her if she tried to leave him.

Sending the videos to her parents was the least awful of these. There was mention of the police, leading to inevitable imprisonment and hints of terrible reprisals by the film distributors who seemed to be on a par with the Mafia.

' 'Not sure', what do you mean?' he asked angrily. Haven't I done well for you so far, getting you these parts, not to mention the money?'

'I suppose so.'

He made it sound like her movie career was progressing towards a starring role in Spielberg's next epic. Instead, it was altogether more sinister.

She was hardly listening as he explained to her finer points of what he called 'bondage videos' and how they could make twice as much money as straight films.

'You won't get hurt,' he promised her. 'Everything's faked. The blood's all tomato ketchup.' He omitted to mention that there were people willing to pay thousands for genuine 'snuff movies'. He didn't think she was quite ready for it. Yet.

'Do I have to?'

'The studio's free tomorrow.' He played his final card of persuasion. 'It's worth £500 to each of us, and you do love me don't you, darling?' and he kissed her gently on the lips.

'All right,' she conceded. 'But you won't let them hurt me, will you?'

'Of course not,' he lied.

He dropped her off at the end of her road as usual. It was 10.25 pm. Linzi's mind was in turmoil as she walked slowly towards her home. She was frightened of what was going to happen to her if she made the film. Gordon had mentioned her being tied up. What if he wasn't able to help her once the film started? As always, too, she worried about who might eventually see the video and recognise her. But if she didn't turn up, Gordon would only seek her out and what then?

She closed her eyes and tried to remember the prayers she used to say at Sunday School. If God were real, surely he would save her.

But who believed in God anymore?

There was only one, desperate, solution.

If she died, nobody could hurt her. For the first time, Linzi thought of suicide. Her mother kept packets of sleeping tablets by her bedside. She could take these and leave a note saying she was worried about her GCSE mocks that were next month. No one would ever know about the films. It would all be over.

She quickened her steps. In that instant she'd made up her mind and she felt exhilarated with the illusion of freedom.

She didn't dare to think of the heartache her parents would suffer, finding the body of their beloved only daughter, never to reach her fifteenth birthday.

As she came up to her gate, a car pulled up alongside the kerb and a man wound down the window and spoke to her. 'Linzi Pennington?'

She jumped, startled. 'Who are you?'

Linzi Pennington didn't know it but her prayers had been answered. Her moment of divine intervention was at hand, although the middle-aged driver in the ex-army greatcoat bore little resemblance to any Saviour she'd ever seen in her Scripture books.

'Detective Chief Inspector Glass, Scotland Yard.' He held out an I.D. card. 'Would you mind stepping into the car, miss?'

4

Glass jumped out of the driver's seat and ushered Linzi into back of the car, following her in and shutting the door. WPC Ngoomba remained in the front passenger seat.

The detective wasted no time in getting to the point. Producing a more lurid photograph than the one he had shown Mrs. Pennington, he thrust it under her Linzi's nose. 'I'd like you to tell me about this,' he said.

When she saw the picture, Linzi burst into tears. This was all her worst nightmares come true, the police, her parents, jail . . .

'Where did you get it?'

'Available at all good newsagents,' said Glass, unkindly. 'I want to know the name of the man who took the picture.'

She didn't dare say his name. Her love for him wasn't so blind that she didn't realise Gordon Nightingale could be cruel and ruthless if crossed.

'I . . . I don't know.'

Glass dropped his voice to a confidential whisper. 'Your mother and father haven't had the pleasure of watching a video entitled 'Playground Pets' as yet. If you don't help me, I'm afraid they may get a private showing.'

Linzi sobbed harder. How had they got hold of the film? Gordon had promised it would only be sold in foreign countries. He'd lied to her.

'His name,' persisted Glass.

What could she do? The police were as bad as Gordon was with their threats and blackmail. But the police held the aces. Gordon wasn't here. This policeman had the film and her parents were only yards away.

WPC Ngoomba placed a warning hand on Glass's shoulder to so suggest he went easy with her but the policeman shrugged it off. He knew what he was doing.

'Well?'

'If I tell you, you won't tell my mother?'

'I promise you, she won't see the film,' replied Glass obtusely. It was enough to satisfy the young girl.

'His name's . . . his name's Gordon Nightingale.'

'From round here is he?' The Penningtons lived in Kew.

'No, he's from Shepherds Bush. That's where I met him, at a disco.'

'And how old is Mr. Nightingale?'

'About twenty, twenty one, I think.'

'Can you describe him for me?'

Linzi did her best to furnish him with a reasonable likeness of her lover.

'And it was his idea was it, for you to pose for photos and stuff?'

'He said no-one would see them and he paid me.' She pursed lips defiantly. 'Anyway, he loves me.'

Glass snorted in desperation. Love wasn't an emotion whose path he had often crossed and he never ceased to be amazed at the activities perpetrated under its guise.

'Have you been with him tonight?' She nodded, miserably. 'And when are you seeing him again?'

'Tomorrow. We're . . . ' she stopped.

'Yes?'

'Gordon's hired a studio for us to make another film.'

'Has he By Jove?' An expression of delight lit up Glass's worn features. 'Couldn't be better. What's the address?'

'I don't know. I'm supposed to be meeting him in a pub after school.'

'What time's that?'

'Four o'clock.'

Glass noted down the name and address of the establishment. 'And where does your mother think you'll be?'

'Having tea at a friend's and going to the pictures.'

'Right. I want you to keep that appointment tomorrow, Linzi.'

At this point, WPC Ngoomba interceded. 'Hang on, sir. We can't use the girl as bait. It could be dangerous.'

Glass ignored her. 'I'll have two of my best men with you all the way and I'll be in constant radio contact. As soon as you're in the studio, we'll pounce.' Linzi trembled at the word. What would Gordon do?

'You've no need to worry about your boyfriend,' said the detective, as if reading her thoughts. 'He'll never know it was you who tipped us off and, once we've got him, all your worries will be over.' He didn't mention anything about trials and interfering with witnesses. No sense in scaring her off. 'And now we'd better deliver you safely to your parents.'

He struggled out of the car and went up to the Pennington's front door, leaving the policewoman to escort Linzi in his wake. Mrs. Pennington answered it within seconds.

'Linzi's not back . . . ' She stopped as she saw WPC Ngoomba escorting her daughter up the path.

'A quick word in private, Mrs. Pennington.' He almost pushed her into her own dining room and shut the door behind them.

'It's all a foolish prank,' he lied. 'Linzi's explained everything and there's nothing to worry about. If I were you, I'd say nothing to her, it would only embarrass and upset her if she knew that you knew about the photo.' He still referred to it as if it were a one-off snapshot.

'I see.' Mrs. Pennington was finding the changing situation hard to grasp but anything was welcome that would save her having to discuss matters of a sexual nature with her daughter.

'That's that, then,' said Glass, as the two police officers returned to their car. 'Tomorrow we pick up this Nightingale bloke, and in the meantime, I want you find out if there's any form on him Constable er . . . ' he stopped, unsure quite how to address his companion. 'What do people call you?'

'My friends call me Wendy.' She smiled at his discomfort. 'Possibly because it's my name.'

Sarcasm was wasted on Glass. 'Right, Wendy. Well check him out with Records, find out about any known associates and, with a bit of luck, we'll be one step nearer towards nailing the low life behind this little lot.'

It was eleven thirty as they returned to the

39

station. Glass suddenly remembered that he hadn't rung his daughter to say he wouldn't be in for his dinner. More trouble when he got home, he thought, although she should be used to it with two policemen to look after.

Sue was married to Detective Chief Inspector Robin Knox, a man twenty-five years his junior and a University graduate who'd risen quickly through the ranks to his present position.

Glass, who was sceptical of officers he referred to as 'college boy coppers', nonetheless had been willing enough to move from his rented flat in Shepherds Bush and join the happy couple in their large semi in Chiswick twelve months after the wedding.

Sue Knox had been wary of this arrangement at first but the vagaries of the job meant that one or other of the two policemen was out of the house most of the time, so potentially explosive arguments rarely occurred.

Glass retrieved his beige Morris Traveller from the car park and set off for home. He'd bought the vehicle from an advert in a classic car magazine and took great pleasure in knowing it was appreciating in value whilst his son-in-law's BMW, which vied for space on their drive-in, was costing him thousands a year in depreciation.

Sue greeted him at the door. 'There's a saying I once read on a T-shirt,' she said before he had time to apologise, 'something along the lines of 'Don't look in the oven. Your dinner's in the dog'.'

'Good job we've only got cats then,' replied Glass, leaning down to stroke the grey and white creature that was rubbing itself against his trouser leg and purring loudly.

'Sailor's getting too fat,' warned his daughter. 'All the spoilt meals he gets in this house.'

'No fatter than your Tinker. That animal needs a skateboard to move round the kitchen. Where's Robin?'

'In bed, where do you think?' Her tone bordered on exasperation. 'It is half past twelve in the morning and he's due in at his desk at seven.' She sighed. 'Why didn't I marry somebody ordinary like a stockbroker or a Spanish bull fighter, that's what I want to know? One policeman in the family's bad enough but two.'

As she spoke, she took a casserole dish from the cooker and took it to the table and motioned Glass over. He threw his greatcoat over a chair and went meekly to his place. He knew she worried about her men and didn't

41

like to go to bed till they were both safely home and he was secretly grateful for it.

He tucked into the hot vegetable stew she'd cooked earlier for her husband with suet dumplings and chunks of steak added to his portion. Robin, a devotee of Linda McCartney concoctions, favoured the herb dumplings and quorn.

'What case is he working on at the moment?' he asked as he ate.

'The usual half dozen, I suppose. You know he never talks about them. What about you?'

Glass was quite happy to discuss his cases with anyone who would listen. He reckoned this was how he often obtained most of the information that ultimately enabled him to solve them; from members of the public anxious to put him right about things.

'Well, I've got the Mystery of the Pantomime Cow and who killed him,' he corrected himself, 'or, rather, half of him.'

'I saw that in the paper. *Jack and the Beanstalk* wasn't it? With Harry Hooper? I used to like him when he was in that sitcom on ITV, the one about vicars.'

'That's the chap. Anyway, the poor sod that played the front of Jack's cow got his throat cut. Or was it the back? I forget.'

'One of the cast do you think?'

42

'No idea. I've got Sergeant Moon interviewing them all.'

'How is Moon? Still engaged to Ethel?'

'As far as anybody knows.' Detective Sergeant Moon's long standing engagement was a source of amusement to everyone at the Yard.

'So, you've no idea who did it then?'

'Not so far. We can't find any motive. He lived with the bloke who played the other half of the animal. I'd have had him marked down for the job, lover's tiff or something, but he seemed genuinely distraught. Not unlikeable, either, for a brown hatter.'

Sue said nothing. She found it wiser not to challenge her father's prejudices.

'In the meantime, I'm now lumbered with Scotland Yard Detective's Teenage Goddaughter in Blue Film Scandal.'

'Whatever are you on about?'

'Trevor Evans. The Porn Squad confiscated this blue video from somewhere and it turned out his goddaughter was one of the stars.'

'Oh god, he's strict Chapel too, isn't he.' She laughed.

'Not so funny, Sue, when you know she's only fifteen.'

Her smile vanished. 'You're joking. How did she get mixed up in that?'

'Led astray by her dodgy boyfriend.' He

43

scraped his dish and smacked his lips approvingly. 'By God, that was good. I never lived like this in that flat of mine. Is there a pudding?'

'No there isn't. Not at one in the morning. Have you caught him, then?'

'No, but I will tomorrow. It's the people behind him I want though.'

'I thought all this hardcore porn stuff came in from abroad?'

'Most of it does and, with modern communications, there's little we can do to stop it anymore. On the other hand, if there's an organisation making them here in Britain then I want them.'

Sue Knox had seen that determined look before and knew it meant trouble for someone.

5

It was nine fifteen on Thursday morning.

Detective Chief Inspector Knox sat in his office at New Scotland Yard and contemplated the report on his desk.

The body of a fifteen year old girl, found the previous morning in an alley nearby a peep show joint in Soho, had been identified as Judy Whay, a schoolgirl from Bath who had been missing from home for three days. She'd been sexually assaulted and strangled before being dumped in the alley where she was discovered by a bakery worker on his way to the early shift.

More disturbing was the fact that the murder was linked to two other similar killings that had taken place in Buxton and Llandudno within the last six months, both victims being teenage girls who had suffered similar horrific injuries.

Now Scotland Yard had been called in.

The first victim had died back in March, a sixteen year old Buxton shop assistant called Emma Turner who was missing for four days before her body was found on the bleak, snow-covered moors two miles from

45

the Cat and Fiddle pub.

Horrific bruises confirmed she had been sexually assaulted before being strangled.

Several local youths had been questioned, including her regular boyfriend, a fork lift truck driver from Macclesfield, but no arrests had been made.

A security video showed the boyfriend waiting for her at a town centre shopping centre, confirming his story that he waited half an hour for her before leaving alone when she failed to turn up. He never saw her alive again.

Tyre tracks round the area where the body was found were identified as belonging to a Ford Mondeo but the vehicle was never traced.

The next death came in September. A fifteen-year-old schoolgirl, Maxine Berry, went to an eighteenth birthday party at a function room above a pub in Llandudno. Several of her friends attended the party to which Maxine travelled alone by bus as she lived in Deganwy on the opposite side of the town.

Over sixty people at the party confirmed she was there until midnight when the disco finished playing and she called a taxi from a public phone box by the bar.

The general unreliability of eyewitnesses

was clearly demonstrated when police asked for a description of the car that arrived to pick her up.

Eight people confirmed they had seen the car, none had taken the number, but four thought it was a Vectra, two a Mondeo, and one an Escort. The colours suggested ranged from dark green to blue whilst the last witness swore it was a black taxicab. It was nothing more than the police expected.

The real taxi pulled up five minutes later by which time Maxine was well on her way to her grisly destination.

She was not seen again until firemen pulled her body out of a burnt out workshop on an industrial estate near Colwyn Bay a week later.

Luckily for the forensic people, by some unlikely chance the body had not been consumed by the flames as had obviously been intended, and a post mortem was quickly able to establish that she had been strangled before being taken to the workshop.

But not before sustaining injuries that made even the experienced pathologist blanch.

Any clues that had been found had so far failed to produce a suspect. A hair lodged under the dead girl's thumbnail had opened up the possibility of identification by DNA testing, but it proved to belong to a dog, possibly a border collie.

Three months later, despite extensive enquiries by the Welsh police, Maxine Berry's murderer remained at large.

Now the killer seemed to have struck once more, this time in London, with the murder of Judy Whay. Another strangulation with hideous mutilations markedly similar to those of the earlier victims.

'We're convinced that this is the work of a serial killer,' the Commander of Scotland Yard had told ITV cameramen in a dramatic interview for 'News at Ten' the previous evening, in which he appealed for members of the public not to shield a dangerous man who would probably kill again.

'There is no evidence of gain in these murders. This is a man,' he quickly corrected himself, 'a person, who kills for pleasure.'

The media had eagerly grasped this scenario and the morning tabloids carried banner headlines referring to 'The Terror Reign of The Spa Killer', forgetting, in their anxiety for a good label, that Llandudno's waters came from the sea not from beneath the ground.

Robin Knox pushed the report away and sighed. The department was understaffed, budgets were tight and violent crime was rising, despite statistics to the contrary.

Knox knew these were doctored to reassure a worried public, many of whom were frightened to leave their homes at night.

He picked up one of two telephones on his desk and dialled a number. 'Otis Ellis please. It's Det. Chief Inspector Knox, Metropolitan Police.'

He waited while he was put through. 'Otis? Robin Knox. Can you spare an hour later this morning? I've got a case I'd like to discuss with you.'

Otis Ellis was a psychology professor at a London University who had attained a certain reputation as an expert in criminal profiling. He and Knox had worked together successfully on a previous occasion.

In all three major cases in which the police had sought his services, Ellis had correctly identified the characteristics of the suspects subsequently arrested for the crimes.

'Not the Bath schoolgirl by any chance?'

'How did you guess?'

'I saw it on the news last night. Yes, I can spare an hour. Shall we say eleven o'clock?'

They met at the Wig and Pen by Aldwych, once the second home of Fleet Street journalists before they moved out to Docklands, and now filled with assorted members of the law profession. Walter Glass had first introduced Knox to the establishment, being one of it's longest serving members.

'It's all in the file,' explained Knox as the two men took their drinks to a quiet table in the corner. 'There have been three victims so far that we know of, all with similarities that lead us to believe it's the work of one man.'

Otis Ellis opened the file and glanced through the papers. He was a tall, bespectacled black man in his late thirties. He wore a dark blue suit with matching shirt and tie and brightly polished black shoes and could have been mistaken for a city banker. He had a deep voice yet spoke softly and with a clipped public school accent which belied his East London origins.

Ellis replaced the papers and turned to Knox. 'These are particularly disturbing crimes,' he said. 'I notice the details of the injuries were not released to the papers.'

'The fact that the clitoris was severed in each case before death, you mean? Yes, we felt that it would serve no purpose. It would only alarm the public and we daren't risk the chance of possible copycat crimes.'

'Quite right.'

'What significance would you attach to it?'

'Obviously it is highly symbolic, like a

50

woman amputating a man's genitals. It's the action of a man who fears women and this fear has developed over the years into a psychopathic hatred. The amputation alone could have caused death from shock.'

'You'd agree, would you, that someone who has killed three times in this fashion is likely to kill again?'

'Without a doubt,' said Ellis. 'You're looking here at a man who is unable to interact socially with the opposite sex. He's probably the victim of abuse or comes from a home where he never received enough love and affection to raise his own self esteem.'

'How will he appear to other people?'

'He's going to be an outsider in society, a loner.'

'But will he have enough grasp on things to, say, hold down a job?'

'Oh yes. Depends on the job, of course. He won't fit into a team situation and is unlikely to be successful at man-management. Maybe self-employed, running his own business.'

'Probably an intelligent man, then?'

Ellis smiled. 'You sound surprised Robin. Intelligence doesn't go hand in hand with morality, you know. I mean, look at Nero. He played a wonderful violin.'

'Okay, I take your point Otis.'

'He could be something like a freelance

sales representative, someone who works on his own to a large degree and, given the distance between the crimes, a person who moves around the country a good deal.'

'Maybe a long distance lorry driver?'

'Yes. Or even, of course, a retired person with free time on his hands although crimes of this nature are nearly always committed by men under fifty. By that age, the sexual urges of even the most enthusiastic perverts tend to become assuaged by the passage of time.'

'I was hoping for a bit longer than that,' commented Knox who had been known as a playboy in his bachelor days. They both laughed, then Knox became serious again. 'But he could be quite successful at his job which would help disguise any untoward actions he might make?'

'Without a doubt. A successful face to the public but behind the mask . . . ' He left the words unfinished.

'Why schoolgirls, do you think?'

'For a start, they're inexperienced so they present no threat to his masculinity. Then their lack of physical strength would prevent them from putting up much of a defence.'

'They're so far apart, the killings. From Yorkshire to Wales and now this girl, found in London but possibly killed in Bath. Do you think the towns are significant?'

52

'If they are, I can't think why. He probably just happened to be there on those occasions.'

'A tragic case of being in the wrong place at the wrong time for those girls.'

'Quite so.'

'What about marriage? Are we looking for a single man?'

'Or a divorced one. Like we said, he obviously has trouble sustaining relationships so I suspect he will be on his own or possibly living with his mother or maybe a sister and her family.

'So you don't think he's another Fred West where the wife's in it with him?'

'That's a complete one-off, the West case. In any case, all the victims there were buried in the family homes. This fellow moves around.'

'So, we're looking for a man, probably living alone, travelling with his job and likely to be in his what, early thirties do you think?'

'Between twenty and forty, nothing more specific at this stage.'

'How about a criminal record?'

'Very possibly. Something like petty theft or maybe minor sexual crimes like indecent assault, exposing himself, that sort of thing.'

'That cuts the search down to a few

hundred thousand,' said Knox with a bitter smile. 'A mammoth task. At least the Yorkshire Ripper confined himself pretty much to one area.'

'If you assume Peter Sutcliffe committed all the so-called Ripper crimes.'

Knox said nothing. He didn't want to be drawn into that argument.

'Have you no clues?'

'Oh yes. We've established the same knife was used in each case but we haven't found it.'

The black man looked grave. 'He's probably keeping it for his next victim.'

'The trouble is, we're not at the stage yet where we can bring in suspects and until we can find some link between the victims . . .'

'You think there could be one?'

'Don't you?'

'No. I'd say they were random killings.'

'If you're right, that makes my job even harder.' Knox stood up. 'Thanks a lot for coming, Otis. Once we get some suspects in, at least I'll have some idea of what we're looking for.' He led the way to the exit. 'How's your team getting on this season?' Ellis was a West Ham United supporter.

'Doing well, Robin. Hartson and Kitson up front, knocking the goals in. Can't say the same for your father-in-laws lot.' Glass's team, Queens Park Rangers were languishing in the lower reaches of the First Division.

Robin Knox preferred cricket.

They parted at The Strand and Knox walked back to New Scotland Yard thinking about the case.

There was not one clue to suggest where the killer might be based. Checks on known sex attackers in the areas had produced nothing.

Judy Whay had always lived in Bath and it was a mystery to her parents how her body had turned up in Soho.

She had left home on Sunday morning to stay for a week at a friend's in Newquay. On Monday evening, the friend had rung Judy's home to see if she was in and was surprised to find she was supposed to be with her in Cornwall.

Her parents immediately alerted the local police and Judy was registered as a missing person but within forty-eight hours, her body had turned up near Old Compton Street and Scotland Yard had a major case on its hands.

Judy Whay was victim number three and the time between murders was getting shorter. How long before the fourth victim?

6

Knox arrived back at his office as Glass was coming along the corridor.

'I believe you're heading the hunt for The Spa Killer,' said the older man, 'or so the papers tell me.'

Robin grimaced. 'I'm looking for a serial killer, Walter, whatever name he goes under.' He could never bring himself to call his wife's father, Dad.

'Any joy so far?'

Robin shook his head. 'No. Three bodies, similar mutilations, hundreds of miles apart and no obvious links between any of them. I've just had a meeting with Otis Ellis, you know, the criminal profiler.'

'I know who he is,' barked Glass dismissively.

'He reckons he can build up a decent picture of the man we're looking for.'

'Bollocks. It's all modern chicanery that psychology guff. If you want to find your killer, get a few Bobbies on the beat and listen to what the people on the streets are saying. That's how you catch criminals, through informers, not this scientific mumbo jumbo.'

'How are you getting on with Trevor Evans' godchild and the blue films?' Knox thought it prudent to change the subject and he'd heard all about Glass's infamous night at the Compton Road Welfare and Social Club. It was the talk of the Yard.

'Fine. I'm off this afternoon to pick up the director then we'll find out which illustrious studio they're coming from.'

'You've found him already?'

'Certainly have. I'll have him in the cells by teatime.' Glass had taken the spoiling of his Christmas party personally and was looking forward to extracting revenge on the man who had made the *Playground Pets* video. 'Either that or in the hospital. Depends on how hard I hit him.'

★ ★ ★

Gregory Oliver was finding life alone very difficult. Max's body had been taken away and he had spent the whole of Tuesday sitting in his winged armchair whilst a succession of forensic technicians and policemen took the flat apart.

He was questioned by a Detective Sergeant who took a statement from him confirming the time he returned from the shops to find the body of his partner.

57

He provided bank statements for both himself and Max and instructed his solicitors to allow the police to inspect their wills.

'No,' he told the sergeant, 'we didn't have any enemies. We were not in debt. We had no other lovers. We were happy together.'

On Wednesday, the police left him alone but the Stage manager at the theatre phoned to ask when he would be returning to the pantomime. A stagehand had been recruited to act as understudy for the back end of the cow, if the role deserved such a title.

Gregory hesitated but something was muttered about the show having to go on so he told them he would be in the following evening.

On Thursday morning, he walked to the shops at the end of the road. He needed some paracetamol for his headache and there was a chemist a few hundred yards round the corner.

He bought a newspaper at the Eight till Late and a frozen chicken and vegetable pie for his lunch.

He read the headlines as he walked slowly along the pavement back to the flat so didn't notice the grey Metro mount the kerb and hurtle towards him.

It was an Asian lady, wheeling a buggy containing a small child, who averted the disaster. She was walking a few paces behind Gregory, about to overtake him on the shop side, when she saw the approaching car and leapt forward to drag the ageing actor towards the wall. The car roared off before either of them had chance to register it.

Gregory thanked the lady profusely for saving his life. He blamed himself for reading the paper and not looking where he was going. It didn't occur to him that it might not have been an accident.

That someone had deliberately tried to kill him.

∗ ∗ ∗

Linzi Pennington was very apprehensive about her after-school appointment with Gordon Nightingale at the film studio. What would happen after the raid if he found out it was she who had informed the police?

She didn't pay much attention in class that day. 'What's up?' asked her friend Clover as they ate their beefburgers in the canteen at lunchtime. 'You seem upset about something.'

'Nothing, I'm all right,' snapped Linzi. 'I'm just not hungry.' She put the half-eaten substance back on the plate with a grimace.

'Ugh! God knows what's in those things, they're vile.'

'You've never complained before. Are you sure nothing's the matter?'

'I told you, I'm fine. Just leave me alone will you?' But she was visibly shaking when she went to meet her lover at the prescribed hostelry at four o'clock. Another thought was troubling her. What if Gordon spotted the police straight away and realised she'd betrayed him?

Nightingale noticed her disquiet immediately. 'What's the matter, sweetheart? You're not usually nervous.'

'It's this torture idea,' she lied. 'Being tied up and everything. What if they do really hurt me?'

Nightingale put his arm round her. 'Do you think I'd ever let anyone harm you, darling? I've told you, it's all faked. Look, why don't you get a couple of drinks down you, that'll make you feel better.'

She looked round the pub whilst he got the drinks, trying to spot the policemen who were supposed to be guarding her. She couldn't see anyone who fitted the bill until she realised that the girl in the corner chatting intimately with a black man was Wendy Ngoomba. That gave her some reassurance.

'Here we are, a double gin and tonic.' Gordon put a tall glass in front of her and she took a gulp.

'What will I have to do?' she asked, desperately making conversation in case he noticed they were being watched.

'The director will tell you all that,' he assured her. 'Don't worry.'

'Will I have to do it with other people again?' She remembered the cameraman from the last film.

'Probably, but I'll be there as well.' As if that made everything all right.

As soon as she'd finished her drink, he jumped up. 'Right, let's go. Don't want to keep them waiting.'

Gordon had his car on a meter a few yards down the road. As they pulled away, she couldn't stop herself from turning round to see if the two police officers were in sight but she could see no-one.

Linzi felt a terrible fear grip her. The police had let her down. They'd lost her. Now she was on her own. She no longer believed Gordon when he said she wouldn't be harmed but there was no way out for her. She would have to make the film and be subjected to the pain and the shame.

Nothing could save her now.

The drive to the studio took only fifteen

minutes. He parked in a yard at the back of a Victorian terrace of shops with three floors of flats above and they entered through a middle door which led straight to some dark stairs. She followed him up.

'This is it.' He paused at an unmarked door along a corridor on the third floor and rang a bell.

The man who opened the door was short and stocky and of Maltese origin. He merely grunted and led the way into a large room equipped with floodlights, projectors and camera equipment. It all looked very professional to Linzi. A far cry from the last film which had been shot at Gordon's house.

What scared her, however, was the set, which was constructed as a cell with iron bars. There were stocks, chains, a gallows, various whips and a selection of leather costumes.

'Looks like something from The Three Musketeers, eh?' smiled Gordon cheerfully. 'Don't worry. It's all for show.'

Linzi was despatched to a cloakroom to change into her costume, which turned out to consist of just a half-cup leather bra and matching thong. She was trembling as she fastened the straps.

The Maltese man, who seemed to be both

director and cameraman, led her to the 'cell' and made her lie down, face upwards, fixing her legs and arms apart to rings fixed in the floor.

At this point, her two co-stars put in an appearance. Both were naked. The first was a man in his twenties, six feet four inches tall with a muscular oiled body from which jutted a penis the size of a family-size cucumber.

The thought of this entering her didn't terrify the young schoolgirl as much as the demonic look in the man's eyes, which hinted at madness.

By contrast, the second man was grotesque. He looked well over seventy with white hair on his chest and flabby wrinkled thighs. Happily, his personal regions were hidden from view by his huge, hanging belly

The Maltese man switched on the lights and the Schwarzeneggar look-alike picked up a horsewhip from the floor and approached the horizontal figure staked out in the cell.

'Take One,' murmured the director and he set the cameras in motion as his leading actor stepped forward and brought the whip down viciously on Linzi's naked body.

She screamed with pain and looked round desperately for Gordon but he was nowhere in the room. She writhed from side to side trying to free her arms and legs but to no avail.

She closed her eyes and prayed someone would rescue her.

At this point, the old man stepped forward, sank arthritically to his knees and endeavoured to insert his flaccid member into Linzi's mouth, pulling her hair to jerk her head back. At the same time as his companion lifted up his arm to strike her again.

The whip never landed. There was a thunderous crash and the door flew open to reveal two men in anoraks, T-shirts and jeans.

' 'Police,' shouted the first man. 'Nobody move.'

The Maltese man immediately ran for the door but the first detective threw himself at him and hurled him brutally against the wall where his head smashed against the door frame and he collapsed unconscious onto the floor.

Linzi, who had never seen officers of the law in action before, looked on aghast. Her co-star turned round, whip in hand and lashed out at the other policeman, catching him on the side of the face and sending him staggering.

The first policeman wheeled round and landed two punches far enough below the actor's navel to have disqualified him under the Marquis of Queensberry's rules. As the actor doubled up with pain, the policeman followed though with a sharp knee to his unprotected groin and the thespian slumped in agony to the floor.

Meanwhile, the old man, having abandoned his quest for septuagenarian sex, quivered in a corner, pleading with the intruders not to hit him in view of his advanced age and suspect heart condition but the officers were too busy releasing Linzi Pennington from her bonds to bother about him.

'Sorry, we were a bit late,' apologised her rescuer with a smile. 'The traffic's a bit dodgy this time of day. You go and put yer clothes on, luv.'

Linzi needed no second bidding. She ran to the cloakroom and pulled on her clothes. Shaking with relief and shock, she was about to ask what had happened to Gordon when the door opened and Detective Chief Inspector Glass entered, pushing in front of him a sorry figure covered in blood and bruises.

'Look what I found in the corridor,' he beamed. 'Cecile B. deMille himself.' Glass still lived in the so-called Golden Age of the Cinema. 'I'm afraid he fell downstairs and hurt himself.'

'I'll have you for this, it's assault that's what it is,' spluttered Gordon Nightingale who didn't seem quite as threatening now as he held his hand to his nose which seemed to be hanging at an odd angle.

'Nothing to what you'll be getting later.' Glass smiled at him threateningly. 'Bennett, take them all down to the station and charge them and don't forget the girl.'

Glass managed to wink at Linzi to let her know this last bit was for Nightingale's benefit, to protect her possible future reprisals.

Detective Sergeant Bennett, meanwhile, was having problems reviving two of his charges but they eventually recovered enough to be dragged, handcuffed and dazed, down the stairs to where two police cars were waiting on the double yellow lines outside.

'What'll happen to Gordon?' Linzi asked as she sat in the back of the second car next to the detective. WPC Ngoomba was in the front passenger seat alongside her companion from the pub.

'We'll charge him and he'll get bail but we'll get an injunction on him not to approach you. We'll also let him believe you're being charged. But, you'll be quite safe now, Linzi, believe me. We'll throw the book at your Mr. Nightingale. He'll go down for a good stretch, no mistake. Judges aren't keen on sex crimes and I could write a book about what'll happen to him and his chums in prison. The other inmates won't be too fond of them.

Linzi could almost have felt sorry for her erstwhile boyfriend until she remembered the events in the studio and realised that he'd lied to her. They had had every intention of hurting her.

'What I want now,' Glass was saying, 'are the men behind him who distribute this filth.'

7

The three men from the film studios looked like extras from *Casualty* as they slumped in their respective cells.

A police doctor had been called to attend to the injuries they had sustained 'while resisting arrest', as Glass later described it in his report. 'Covering my back' he explained to his colleagues.

They were then brought in turn to an interview room to be questioned.

The Maltese proprietor of the studio affected to speak little English but he confirmed that he owned the premises and rented them out to interested parties who wanted to make their own films.

He admitted, when pressed, that he sometimes provided 'actors' on request to help out when needed in a particular production and he maintained that the bondage equipment was just one of many sets available to prospective hirers.

He had sincerely believed that the girl, Linzi, was an actress and was horrified to learn that she was really a schoolgirl who had been duped into taking part in the film although he was sure that she would have come to no harm.

Sergeant Evans, who was the required other officer at the interview, managed to restrain himself from rushing across the room to kick the prisoner's bandaged head.

'Who do you send the film to?' snarled Glass but the Maltese insisted, in surly broken English, it was not his film to send anywhere.

'I just provide the studio. He take the film, that Mr. Nightingale.'

The interrogation of the two 'actors' proved just as unsatisfactory. The elderly man whined on about his angina and warned the officers that any undue stress could bring on a heart attack at any time without warning.

He swore he'd originally been asked to take part in a documentary feature about the Roman Games. He was unable to give a reason why he had to appear stark naked in the production. They had just told him that 'that was how the Romans were' and he accepted it.

As for the girl, he supposed she was brought in to add a bit of sauciness like they did in films nowadays. He thought she was a genuine actress.

He was unable to account for the fact that

he had attempted to engage in fellatio with the girl, other than 'something had come over him'.

The leading actor, the Schwarzeneggar clone, made no secret of his calling. He was a star of porn flicks and proud of it.

'Big Ben, they call me. I'm a stud for hire. Fellas like me aren't easy to find.' When Glass probed further, Ben patiently explained to him that many men suffered from detumescence when obliged to perform before the cameras but he himself had never had that problem.

'The bigger the audience,' he boasted, 'the more I rise to the occasion.'

'Really?' The Chief Inspector was not impressed. 'And I suppose the excitement of beating up and raping a helpless under-age schoolgirl also adds to your virility?'

'Hang on a minute.' The prisoner's demeanour changed at the mention of 'rape' and 'under-age'. 'I never knew how old she was. And I didn't rape her. I just pretended to hit her, that's all.'

'We've got the doctor's report,' pointed out Glass, 'with details of the bruises where you 'pretended' to hit her.'

'What about the doctor's report where you pigs assaulted me, eh? Police brutality that

70

was. I'm lucky I've still got my fuckin' bollocks.'

Glass almost smiled. 'Pity you didn't lose them then you could have sued us for loss of trade.'

'And I didn't know she was under age. Or at school.' He became very excitable but the two officers remained silent. 'Are you listening to me? I tell you, I was led to believe she was like me, did this for a living.'

'Don't tell me,' sighed Glass. 'You thought she was a genuine actress?'

'That's right. I did. And you can't prove otherwise.'

'The trouble is,' Glass said, as the prisoner was escorted back to his cell, 'we can't.'

'We can get him for assault, surely? Trevor Evans couldn't believe that the animal could get off scot-free.

'Depends who his brief is. We might get him on a blue films rap but nothing much had happened by the time we arrived. You can see as bad as that on television these days. And that's only in the soaps.'

'What about Nightingale?'

'Now he's the one I really want, the bastard who first seduces these innocent young girls. Also, of course, he's the one person who can lead us to the scum who

71

distribute the films. We'll have him in next.'

'I've told you, I don't know who buys the films.' Gordon Nightingale looked a pathetic figure in the interview room. The bandage covering half his face was now nearly fully scarlet. Gone was the bravura that he exhibited in front of teenage girls like Linzi Pennington. 'I send them off to this address and the cash comes back by registered letter.'

'The address being this post office box number?' Glass studied an envelope that Nightingale had given him. It had a postcode in the West End.

Nightingale nodded sullenly.

'Himmler Films,' read the detective. 'Nice to know that not all you entrepreneurs are Eurosceptics.' The political reference was lost on Gordon Nightingale. 'At a guess I'd say somewhere in Soho, wouldn't you?'

The defendant shrugged his shoulders. 'Who's to say? Why don't you ask the postman?'

'Because I'm asking you, sunshine.' Nightingale shrugged again as if he didn't regard the question as worth answering.

'You see that man in the corner?' Glass pointed to Sergeant Evans, who was the required other officer present at the interview. 'He's Linzi's godfather. If I leave him alone with you while I go for a pee, there's a good chance when I come back he'll have cut your dick off. Which might put paid to your film career sooner than you intended.'

'You can't touch me. I'll get the police complaints people onto you.'

'The trouble is, they're run by the police as well,' sighed Glass. 'It's a bit like having the opposition goalkeeper doubling as the referee.' He walked over to the tape recorder and poked at the controls. 'Interview interrupted whilst suspect attends toilet. Oh dear, I seem to have forgotten to switch the thing on.' Suddenly, he grabbed Nightingale by the back of the neck and his fist thudded into the youth's Adams Apple. 'Now talk.'

The youth choked. Glass switched the tape on. 'Interview with Gordon Nightingale timed at nineteen hundred hours. Present are Detective Chief Inspector Glass and Detective Sergeant Evans.' He turned to the suspect. 'Would you tell me, Mr. Nightingale, where I might find the people who distribute your films?'

The youth coughed, still trying to recover his breath. The bloodied bandage slipped a further inch down the bridge of his broken nose. 'I don't know. It was an advert in the paper.'

73

'What?'

'Honestly. Nothing more than that. 'Glamour photos and amateur videos wanted', it said. Well, I sent up some ones I'd taken of Linzi,' He looked away from Sergeant Evans as he mentioned the teenager's name, 'and they got in touch with me.'

'How?'

'They wrote to me asking if we'd like to take part in a film.'

'The one entitled *Playground Pets*?'

'I think that was what they called it.'

'What was the address on the letter?'

'There wasn't one. It was the box number.'

'And you're telling me that Linzi was willing to take part in this film?'

'I'll say she was.' He smirked and Trevor Evans had to restrain himself from following Glass's example. 'She liked the money didn't she? They all did.'

'Don't worry. We'll be asking you for the names and addresses of the other two girls, later. In the meantime, let's go back to yesterday's epic. We've been told that you organised the actors and gave them their instructions.'

'They come in the post.'

'What do?'

'The scripts. Himmler Films send me the scripts, give me the numbers of the actors and I make the film.'

'And they pay you.'

'S'right.' Nightingale smirked, evidently pleased with his business acumen.

'Except that you have to find your own actresses, under-age schoolgirls, because that's what the perverts who watch this filth want to see.'

'They don't object.'

'Until the films get nasty and they find out they're going to get hurt. I suppose you'll tell me Linzi was enjoying what was happening this afternoon?'

'Of course.'

'Funny. I thought she seemed somewhat upset.'

'No, she was acting wasn't she? Pretending to be hurt, like. Did well didn't she? You could almost believe she was in pain.' He was becoming cocky but Glass's next sentence altered his new-found confidence.

'I'm going to see you get out on bail, son, and then I'm going to find the people from Himmler Films and let them know how co-operative you've been. Naming names, turning Queen's evidence, that sort of thing. I don't expect they'll be too happy with you and I'm afraid we haven't got the manpower to provide you with round the clock protection. However, if at any time you feel in danger, do feel free to dial 999 and hope a patrol car will reach you in time.'

Nightingale's face turned white. 'You wouldn't do that?'

'Sometimes they can be on the spot within two hours. Almost as quick as the AA.'

'But they'll kill me.'

'Possibly,' agreed Glass. 'I find criminals have a much greater sense of justice about these matters than magistrates do. You just can't rely on them to come up with a sentence that acts anything like a deterrent. But I'm sure your colleagues at Himmler Films will know how to deal with traitors.'

Nightingale didn't speak.

'So, for the last time, save me the trouble and tell me their address?'

'There wasn't one. I told you, it was just the box number you saw on the envelope.'

'Right, that's it.' Glass stood up. 'Take him back to the cells.'

The youth's nerve snapped. 'Wait a minute. I'll tell you.'

'Too late. Sergeant Evans! Lock him up.'

Nightingale started to scream. 'No, I'll tell you, I will.'

Glass resumed his seat. 'Just in time for dinner. All right. Make a note of the address Sergeant, then take him back down for the night.'

'Bastard,' breathed Nightingale as the Chief Inspector opened the cell door, but the policeman's parting words made the youth cower.

'Tomorrow, I'll be taking a little trip out to Soho.'

8

'I enjoyed that,' said Glass, pushing away his empty plate and wiping his greasy chin with a paper napkin. 'What was it?'

It was seven o'clock and he was back at home with his daughter and her husband, having eaten a huge helping of Sue's home cooking.

'Oh, thanks,' remarked his daughter. 'That says a lot for my cooking. 'What was it?' indeed! It was quorn in peppercorns and pineapple if you want to know?'

'It wasn't?' Glass put his hand to his mouth involuntarily.

Sue laughed. 'No, you're all right. Yours was chicken, ours was the quorn.'

'Thank God for that. I don't want any of that artificial rubbish in my stomach.'

'It'd do you more good than the stuff you eat. All those pork pies full of nitrates and gallons of caffeine-soaked tea every day, not to mention the amount of alcohol you get through.'

'At least I've given up smoking.'

'Only because they don't make Craven A cork tipped anymore.'

Robin Knox listened contentedly to this banter as he tucked into his quorn. It wasn't often the two men sat down for a meal at the same time but he enjoyed the family occasions and tonight was something of a special one.

'I've got some news for you, Dad.' Sue put a plate of apple pie in front of the detective and a jug of custard. Glass liked his food basic. 'That is to say, WE have some news.'

Glass looked up sharply. 'Hang on. Does that mean what I think it means?'

Sue smiled shyly. Her husband continued with his quorn. 'That depends on what you think it means.'

'I'm not one of the leading lights in the Metropolitan Police for nothing, my girl. When's it due?'

'July 10th.'

Glass broke into a smile. 'That's wonderful.' Sue put her arms around him and he hugged her to him.

'And I thought you weren't sentimental,' said Robin Knox, finishing his meal.

'I suppose you deserve some credit for this.' Glass jumped up and held out his hand to his son-in-law. 'Congratulations, Robin. I'm delighted. Come on, we must open a bottle of champagne.'

'You'll have to settle for claret, it's all we have in.'

Robin went to fetch it leaving father and daughter alone.

'Are you really pleased?' asked Sue, anxiously. 'Babies in the house can be very disruptive, you know. You might get woken up at funny times.'

'I get woken up at funny times already. It's all part of the excitement of being in the Force that they don't mention in the recruitment ads. You should know that by now. What are you going to call it?'

'We haven't decided definitely but we thought maybe Jessica if it's a girl or Ronnie if it's a boy.'

Glass frowned. 'You can't call it Jessie. It's what they call cissy boys.'

'Not in the twenty first century. It's the most popular girl's name in England in 1997 according to the Times.'

'And there's nobody in the country under fifty called Ronnie, and most of them are murderers or football managers.'

'What about Ronnie O'Sullivan the snooker player? He's not fifty.'

'I was thinking more of Ronnie Kray and Ronnie Biggs not to mention Ron Atkinson, Ronnie Moran, Ron Saunders . . . '

'Ron Atkinson didn't kill anyone.'

'Neither did Ronnie Biggs,' pointed out Robin, returning with the claret and three glasses.

'Ask the train driver's wife. She might not agree.'

'What's all this about anyway?' asked Robin uncorking the bottle.

'I just told Dad we might call the baby Ronnie. Perhaps I'd have been safer suggesting Adolf.'

'What's wrong with Jesus Basil then?' and they all collapsed with laughter as Glass poured the drinks. 'To the new member of the family,' he toasted, holding up his glass. 'Whatever the beggar's called.'

They all raised their glasses and drank. A large grey and white cat jumped on the table. 'Sailor wants to join in,' said Glass.

Robin frowned. 'I hope the cats will be all right when the baby comes. I've heard of them jumping onto prams and suffocating the occupants.'

'And lots of kids nowadays are allergic to cats,' added Sue.

'Bollocks,' said Glass. 'How can you be allergic to a cat? It doesn't do anything but eat, shit and purr.'

'It's all to do with asthma. Most children have asthma nowadays apparently and the small cat hairs get up their noses.'

'I tell you who gets up my nose,' said Glass. 'That little sod I had in the cells today. The one that took the dirty videos of Trevor Evans' goddaughter.'

'You've got him then?'

'I said I would. Snivelling little toerag that he is. But it's the people behind the operation I really want. Himmler Films they call themselves.'

Knox shook his head. 'Doesn't ring a bell.'

'Are you still going to Bath tomorrow?' interposed Sue.

Her husband nodded. 'I should be back by evening though.'

'Is this about the schoolgirl they found in Soho?' asked Glass and his son-in-law nodded.

'I'm going to interview her parents and her school friends. Somebody might know something without them realising it. I'd like to know how she ended up in London.'

'And you're sure it's the work of this serial killer?'

'Not much doubt. The injuries were the same. Must be a sadist who did it.'

'I heard about the circumcisions. I suppose your friend Otis is looking for a mentally disturbed transsexual doctor with Jewish blood who slept in his mother's bed till he was fifteen.'

Knox remained tight-lipped. He didn't share his father-in-law's macabre sense of humour.

Sue spoke quickly, recognising a danger point in the conversation. 'How's your pantomime cow enquiry getting on, Dad?'

'It isn't, at the moment. I reckon it'll be somebody at the theatre but as yet, we haven't found a motive. I'm just waiting for somebody to talk. They usually do.'

Robin Knox could not stop an exasperated grunt from escaping his lips. 'All the advances in forensic technology, infra-red photography, DNA profiling, you name it and you still rely on . . .'

' . . . Eddie the Nose,' finished Glass and Sue in unison and they both collapsed with laughter.

Robin tried hard not to be annoyed. 'We'll see who's right,' was all he said. 'We'll see who's right.'

★ ★ ★

The Thursday evening performance of *Jack and the Beanstalk* attracted a full house, there being a last minute rush for tickets by people curious to see the 'death' panto.

They were the sort of people, Gregory Oliver thought, who slowed down on motorways to relish the scenes of carnage after an accident. The newspapers called them 'ghouls'.

Harry Hooper came across to shake Gregory's hand and wish him all the best for the show, consoling him over his loss.

Marsha Flint kissed him and cried. Even Jim Smith who played The Wicked Baron, and who had hardly spoken to either him or Max before, offered him a conciliatory nod.

The young man chosen to be the other half of the cow said little. He wore a pair of close fitting gym shorts and an athlete's singlet. Gregory couldn't help noticing his smooth, hairless chest and felt guilty for being attracted to him with Max still not buried.

'I'll go in the front, shall I?' said the youth, stepping into the costume.

'Well, I usually went at the front but I don't suppose it matters.' Gregory bent forwards and followed him in. A stagehand zipped them up and the 'creature' ambled awkwardly to the side of the stage.

It was in the early part of the second act that the accident happened.

A piece of scenery stored in the flies above the stage came loose without warning and crashed thirty feet down onto the front end of the pantomime cow. The animal collapsed on the ground.

The curtain was brought down as the cast ran to open up the costume. Gregory staggered out backwards, deep in shock, but the boy at the front of the cow lay still, blood pouring from a huge gash at the side of his head.

'Lucky you were at the back, Gregory,' someone said. 'That could have been you.'

The St. Johns Ambulance people, on duty in the theatre, ran backstage to administer first aid to the wounded man.

'He'll live but you'll have to ring for an ambulance and get him to hospital. He needs stitches.'

Meanwhile, someone brought Gregory a chair and the lady who was prompting put a stiff brandy in his hand with the instruction to 'get it down you in one'.

Gregory Oliver felt faint. Only this morning, he had nearly been run over and now this. A horrific thought occurred to him.

Was this really an accident or was somebody trying to kill him?

9

Detective Chief Inspector Knox spent the following morning, which was Friday, travelling to Bath with Detective Sergeant Evans to interview the parents of Judy Whay.

Her father was a lecturer at the University of Bath whilst Mrs. Whay worked for an insurance company in Bristol. They were both at their home on the outskirts of the town awaiting the visit from the Scotland Yard men.

'It's not as if she'd led a wild life,' explained Judy's mother, tearfully. 'She only went out at weekends, usually with a crowd from school.'

'No regular boyfriend then?'

'No. Girls don't seem to form relationships so early these days. They know a lot of boys but they tend to be friends rather than boyfriends.'

'Whereabouts did they go, she and her friends?'

'Oh, to the disco or to one of the local pubs.'

'When she was only fifteen, Mrs. Whay?'

'Let's not be hypocritical here, Chief

Inspector. Everyone knows girls of Judy's age drink. She has wine with us at dinner . . . ' At this, her voice choked. 'She did have wine, I should say.'

Knox saw no point in getting drawn into an argument about under-age drinking and moved on to his next question, the vital one, which concerned the whereabouts of their daughter between the day she left home, ostensibly for Newquay, and the discovery of her body, three days later in Soho.'

'We've no idea. We've been in touch with every one of her friends and none of them had seen or heard from her since Sunday. She'd told them the same story she told us, that she was going to Newquay to stay with Eva. We don't know whether she set off for there or not but Eva certainly wasn't expecting her. When she phoned on Monday to speak to Judy, she was amazed that we were under the impression that Judy was with her in Cornwall.'

'Why did she ring on Monday?'

'I don't understand.'

'If this Eva lived in Newquay, presumably they weren't in touch too often. I wondered what reason Eva had for ringing on that particular day or was it just coincidence?'

'Oh, I see. Well, Eva's family moved to Newquay last year. Judy and she exchange letters every so often and they've spoken on the phone a couple of times, as far as I know. But that's all. I don't know why she rang this week. Just for a chat I suppose. Do you think it could be important?'

'Only inasmuch as Judy would have been relying on Eva not ringing. She'd not bothered to confide in her for an alibi, otherwise Eva wouldn't have rung you. I would think that Judy expected to come home at the end of the week as if nothing had happened and you would have assumed she's been in Cornwall.'

'While all the time she was . . . where?'

Mr. Whay broke in, his voice tired and dispirited. 'We should have rung Eva ourselves and made sure she was expecting Judy.'

'If your daughter had told you she'd arranged the visit, then you'd no reason to doubt her word,' said Knox. 'You can't blame yourself.'

All the same, he thought, if it had been his daughter, he'd have rung to make sure she'd arrived safely.

He didn't voice the obvious question. What was it Judy Whay was planning to do during that week that necessitated her lying to her parents?

'So the last time you saw her was at the station?'

'Temple Mead in Bristol. I gave her a lift there. Her case was heavy so I didn't want her to have to lug it around from station to station.'

'Did you see her get on the train?'

'No. She told me not to wait. The train was running late, you know what Virgin are like, so she was going to buy a magazine and have a drink.' Mr. Whay persisted with his illusions. 'She could, of course, have been planning a surprise visit to Eva's and been waylaid en route.'

Knox didn't give that possibility any credence. 'She was found in London. Did she know anyone there with whom she might have stayed?'

'Not to our knowledge. The local police have already asked us all this, you know, Chief Inspector.'

'I know.' Knox had studied the police reports but they told him nothing. From the day the teenager left home to the time her body was found, there were no sightings of her. 'But sometimes, going over things can trigger some memory you might have forgotten.'

'Do you think she was murdered in London?'

'I cannot say,' Knox replied honestly. 'She'd been dead for over twenty-four hours when she was dumped in the alley, that's all we know for certain. So she didn't die there but the actual killing could have taken place anywhere.'

The two policemen stayed in Bath for lunch at The Pump Rooms where they listened to the string quartet playing excerpts from Mozart whilst they ate.

'What do you reckon?' asked Sergeant Evans of his superior.

'I think she had an assignation with someone, a boyfriend maybe, that she didn't want to tell her parents about.'

'A long assignation. She obviously expected to be gone for a week.'

'Maybe they'd planned a holiday.'

'So who's the boyfriend?'

'I'm hoping we can find that out from her friends.'

The meal finished, they set off for Judy Whay's school where they were allowed to interrupt a geography lesson to address her classmates.

'It is likely,' began Knox, 'that Judy knew the person who killed her. It is also possible that he will kill again which means that, if he is a local man, anyone in this room could be in danger.'

He paused for a moment to let this fact sink in and he could see by the looks of apprehension on some faces his words had had an effect.

'For that reason alone, if any of you can give us even the smallest information about Judy's habits, her associates out of school, boyfriends, anything at all, then please tell us.'

The headmaster provided the officers with an empty classroom and each member of the class was brought in in turn to be questioned. Judy's best friend was a girl called Victoria.

'I honestly don't have a clue where she could have gone.' Victoria was a tall girl with bright red hair that hung over her shoulders. 'She said nothing to me other than she was going to Eva's.'

Victoria knew Eva because they'd all been in the same class through school till Eva left for Cornwall. She didn't think it odd that Judy had gone to stay with her as they'd always kept in touch.

'Judy didn't like to lose people. She still knew people from primary school that I've never seen for years.'

The other girls came forward in turn but the stories were much the same. Her friends seemed surprised at her deception but admitted she was a girl who would sometimes do things to shock people.

'She'd try anything would Judy,' said one

girl. 'She liked a laugh.'

Sergeant Evans wondered if that was what someone might have said about his goddaughter, Linzi and shivered. Young girls today, he thought, had too much freedom.

Girls who didn't know her well, who weren't in her crowd, could offer nothing further but, like everyone in the class, they were very upset.

Only one person offered a glimmer of hope, a girl called Lois who wasn't actually one of Judy's close friends but who used to see her at hockey practice each Friday. They were both in the school first eleven.

'I thought I saw her on Sunday night in a blue Mondeo.'

'Where was that?' asked Knox urgently.

'Twerton, coming up from Bristol, near Rovers football ground.'

'About what time?'

'Oh, at night when the pubs were shutting, about eleven. I was crossing the road with my boyfriend when this car shot past. I didn't think anything at the time but afterwards, when I heard about Judy, I thought it could have been her.'

'How sure are you?'

'I'm not sure. I just said it could have been her. This girl had a lime green top on like Judy's.'

'What about your boyfriend? Did he think it was her?'

'He doesn't know her.'

'She didn't wave or acknowledge you?'

'She didn't look at me. In fact, thinking about it, she looked asleep.'

The two officers exchanged glances. Or drugged. Or dead.

'Did you see who was driving the car? Was it a man?'

Lois thought. 'I think so but I didn't really notice. It was gone in an instant.'

'If anything comes to mind, let me know immediately.' Knox gave her his mobile number.

'So,' murmured Sergeant Evans as they drove back to London on the M4. 'Not much to go on. Do you think any of them are protecting someone?'

Knox shook his head. 'No. Half of them looked terrified. I think Judy Whay had a secret life nobody knew anything about. I'd like to know who was driving that blue Mondeo.'

'We don't know that it was her. Could have been anybody flashing past on a dark night.'

'Even so. It's the only thing remotely like a lead that we've got. Remember, there were Mondeo tyre tracks where the

Buxton's girl's body was found.'

'If this girl's right, then somebody local must be involved because her father dropped her off at the station in the morning and this was night so who had she been with in Bristol all day?'

'What puzzles me is what connection can there possibly be between this kid and a Derbyshire shopgirl?'

'I can't begin to guess, but as far as I'm concerned, the amputations prove we're looking for the same man.'

They travelled a few miles in silence as they both struggled to picture in their minds the circumstances surrounding the girls' deaths then, 'I wonder how Walter Glass is getting on with that bastard who . . . ' Evans struggled to describe the deflowering of his goddaughter, 'you know, with Linzi.'

He needn't have worried. Detective Chief Inspector Glass was looking after his interests only too well.

10

Chief Inspector Glass traced the address of Himmler Films from the post office box number and it turned out to be exactly in the area he'd expected. Soho. It was one of the innumerable sex shops, situated in a side alley near Rupert Street.

Glass's regular assistant, Sergeant Moon, accompanied him on his visit the next morning. They parked their car in a multi-storey in Lexington Street and walked briskly along Beak Street to their destination.

'I don't suppose your Ethel goes in for this sort of gear,' said Glass, pointing to an array of erotic lingerie displayed in a shop window.

Moon coloured. 'Ethel swears by white cotton next to the skin. She says it allows fresh air to reach the pores.' He panted as he tried valiantly to keep up with the Chief Inspector.

'You want to watch that heavy breathing,' remarked Glass. 'It'll get you into trouble.'

They marched on until they came to a tiny shop bearing the sign 'Sex Emporium: Books-Videos-Poppers'. 'Number eleven,' said

Glass. 'This is it,' and he led the way into the shop.

The premises were fitted out with display racks along the walls, all filled with soft porn magazines, and centre units holding stacks of videos. At the back of the shop, hanging on a pegboard display, were items of lingerie of which Moon's fiancée would have undoubtedly disapproved.

The shop assistant sat on a bentwood chair reading the Racing Post. He looked more like a pop star's minder with his shaven head, thin lips and scar down the side of his right cheek. He was at least six foot four tall.

He ignored them until Glass stood in front of his counter, reached over a display of fruit-flavoured condoms and tapped him on the knee.

'Sorry about your alopecia, pal,' he said, sympathetically and flicked his identity card in front of the man's face. 'CID,' he announced. 'We're looking for Himmler Films.'

'Not here, mate.' The man seemed unconcerned. He was in his late thirties and was wearing a cheap black suit that was a size too small for his large frame. His legs were crossed and Glass observed that his shoes needed heeling.

'This is their address?'

'This is where they have their stuff delivered, yes, but they ain't here. They just pick 'em up.'

'I see, an accommodation address. And do they get a lot of this . . . stuff?'

'Tons of it.'

'What is it?'

'I dunno. Don't open it, do I?'

Glass reached across, took the newspaper out of the man's hand and ripped it slowly in half. 'Now, I'll ask you again. Bulky packages are they or just letters?' He dropped the pieces of the Racing Post onto the floor.

The man stared at him. 'You just ripped . . . ' He stopped as he saw the look in the policeman's eye. 'Packages, yeah. Videos and stuff.'

'And how often do they call for these packages?'

'Every day. A courier comes.'

'And you've no idea where he takes them?'

'I don't ask. Some things it's better you don't know.'

'I always thought 'forewarned is forearmed' was a better motto. What time does this courier come?'

'Usually about mid-day.'

Glass consulted his battered chronograph. It was eleven thirty. He held out his hand. 'Where are they?'

97

'What?'

'Come on, today's packages. The postman will have been by now so you'll have got them put by, ready for the courier. Where are they?'

A thin layer of sweat seeped onto the man's bald scalp and was reflected as a myriad of shining dots under the harsh fluorescent light. He looked like he would like to crush Glass's head in his fists but he managed to control himself.

'They've already been picked up.' His voice was hesitant. Glass picked up a cardboard box containing, according to the cover, a ten-inch vibrator with realistic veins and a squeezee bulb and held it aloft. 'Unless you want this appliance to be surgically removed from your throat, I suggest you fetch me today's mail.'

'You friggin' bast . . . ' began the man but he reached under the counter and handed over a pile of Jiffy bags for the chief inspector's inspection. They were addressed to Himmler Films.

'Right,' announced Glass. 'When the courier, as you call him, arrives, you give him the parcels as normal. We'll be watching you so no funny signals. Once he's left, it's down to us, you're out of it, OK? But one word out of place . . . ' the threat was left in the air.

'Right. I just want you out of here.'

'By the way, in case you're wondering what brought us in here, one of your loyal comrades put us on to you, fellow by the name of Gordon Nightingale. Very anxious to talk he was.'

The man said nothing but Glass knew that the name had been noted.

The two policemen spent the next forty five minutes posing as customers, idly inspecting the merchandise, and blending in well with a succession of genuine purchasers, few of whom looked as furtive and shabby as the Chief Inspector.

It was nearly twenty past twelve when a leather-clad youth in a helmet clattered through the shop door. 'Morning George. Bleedin' cold one today, ain't it?'

George gave a quick glance down the shop, saw Glass's eye on him and murmured something inaudible, at the same time handing over the Himmler Film packages to the messenger.

'Let's go, sergeant.' Glass blundered down the aisle and grabbed the youth before he could swivel through the door. 'Police,' he said.

'What the . . . '

'Question time, sonny. Where are you taking that package?'

The youth shook himself free of Glass's grasp.

'Himmler Films, of course. That's what it says on the package. Look.' He thrust the envelopes forward into Glass's lap, throwing the detective off balance whereupon he turned and ran out of the shop.

Sergeant Moon pushed past his superior and chased after him as Glass recovered his balance but he was too late. 'He had a motorbike, sir,' he gasped, 'parked just up the road. He's well away.'

'Shit a sodding brick.' Glass drew in his breath, brushed down his coat and thrust the packages into the pocket of his greatcoat.

'I'm taking these as evidence,' he told the assistant. 'Charges may follow.'

'Nothing to do with me. I've never even opened them.' George smirked. 'I enjoyed your Keystone Cops sketch, officer. You want to try it out in Covent Garden, in the street market, you might make a bob or two.' He laughed as the policeman raised his fist threateningly.

'Come on,' Glass said to Sergeant Moon. 'We'll go and take a look at these epic films, see if we find anything interesting in them.'

They walked back to the car park.

'How are you getting on with the pantomime crowd, by the way?' asked

100

Glass, when they reached their vehicle. 'Any progress?'

'Nothing so far. I've spoken to everyone in the cast, the theatre manager, the backstage crew. Max and Gregory seemed to be quite a popular couple. Certainly nobody, as I can see, had any motive to kill one of them.'

'No sign of the knife?' Moon shook his head. 'And it wasn't a break-in . . . '

'Which brings us back to your initial theory,' vouchsafed Moon. 'The lover.'

'Can't see it,' said Glass in an unashamed volte-face. 'Gregory Oliver was obviously a broken man.'

'Sorry he'd murdered his partner, perhaps?'

'But why would he kill him?'

'Like you said,' Moon was anxious to make clear these were his superior's suggestions, 'a lover's tiff? A crime of passion.'

Glass shook his head. 'He must have upset someone. Outside the theatre, perhaps. What did they do when they weren't working?'

'Not much. The theatre seemed to be their life.'

'Nothing from Forensic, I take it?'

'Not so far. No prints, no sign of the weapon . . . '

'No bodily emissions. Par for the course,' said Glass who had never held a high opinion of the Sherlock Holmes School of Detection.

'Did you check his bank account?'

'Slightly overdrawn but within his credit zone and no unusual sums in or out. Same with his partner.'

Glass sighed. 'It looks like we'll have to wait a little while until somebody talks. In the meantime,' he waved the packages in his hand, 'let's grab some lunch and then we'll settle down to an afternoon at the cinema.'

The 'cinema' was an empty interview room that Glass had commandeered, one equipped with a T.V. set and video player.

As it turned out, the afternoon film show was not enlightening. Glass found himself enduring two hours of mind-numbing pornography that would have blunted the arousal threshold of the most ardent nymphomaniac. Sergeant Moon sat next to him in the darkened operations room, in a state of acute embarrassment.

'It reminds me of when I went to our local fleapit as a lad to see Brigitte Bardot in *And God created women*, ventured Glass. 'Full of dirty old men in long raincoats ready to offer you a mintoe and put their hand in your trousers. Place used to smell of disinfectant and stale semen. I'll tell you what, though,' he added. 'I think we ought to hand over some of that rubbish we've just seen to the RSPCA. They might be able to sue for cruelty to donkeys.'

Moon said nothing. When he'd joined the police force he'd had visions of apprehending international jewel thieves or bravely saving the lives of children in road traffic accidents.

Afternoons watching the unnatural couplings of drug-crazed humans and puzzled farm animals did not match his teenage aspirations.

His superior continued unabated. 'I didn't think much of the music either. I wonder why they don't use something like Beethoven's Fifth as the backing track? I can't stand all that jungle stuff.'

'Nobody we recognised amongst the cast,' commented Moon. 'But at least there were no children.'

'I'd know that redhead again if I saw her. Even with her teeth in. Unfortunately, there was nothing in that little lot to give us any more information on Himmler Films.'

'So what do we do next? Try and follow the messenger again?'

'That could be one possibility,' said Glass who had not yet considered his alternative lines of enquiry.

'There must be a record of them some-where.'

'Must there, Sergeant? Well, put it this way, they're not listed in the phone book and I don't suppose they've bought space in Kelly's Directory.'

'Do you think Nightingale's lying when he says he doesn't know where they are?'

'Oddly enough, I don't. Think about it. They've got a nice little set up here. It's like *Readers Wives* carried to the ultimate extreme. They get these punters hooked into posting them their mildly pornographic videos. Then they start sending out storylines for them to act out, which get progressively nastier but these idiots go along with it . . . '

'And possibly get a kick out of it,' added Moon.

' . . . But all the time, Himmler Films are in the clear as none of the people making the videos know who or where Himmler are. I wonder how many others there are like Gordon Nightingale, doing their dirty work for them?'

'Could be a big operation, a network of agents all across the country and the people behind the operation needn't even be in England. That courier could be relaying everything abroad.'

'In which case, we've no chance,' sighed Glass. 'I can't see Interpol getting too worked up over blue videos.'

'It's probably run by a team of multi-millionaire Continental business men,' said

Moon. 'Or the Mafia.'

Glass sighed. 'Never mind. At least we've got the little sod who seduced Trevor Evans' goddaughter and ruined the Christmas party. That's something.'

Moon nodded and wondered which event had most displeased the inspector.

'Well, I don't know about you,' said Glass, 'but I've had enough of the cinema for one day. Time we had some good wholesome live entertainment. How do you fancy an evening at the pantomime?'

'This evening?' Moon had been looking forward to a quiet night at home with Ethel.

'You surely don't expect a night off with a murder to investigate, Sergeant? Are you forgetting? There's poor Max Cadamarteri rotting in his mortuary drawer and his killer still at large? No, we'll go down to the canteen for some tea then it's South of the river for us. I want to get to the cast before the curtain goes up.'

11

'You still think it's one of the actors then?' asked Sergeant Moon as the two men walked from the car park to the stage door of the theatre.

'Your guess is as good as mine, Moon. I'm lost. Cadamarteri didn't owe money, nothing was stolen from the flat and he'd been in a steady relationship for years so there were no jealous lovers mincing out of the closet. What could he possibly have done to upset someone enough to slit his throat?'

'Perhaps he knew something he shouldn't have.'

'Blackmail, you mean? Good thinking, Sergeant. Could well be. The victim goes round to shut him up rather than pay up. So who in this cast has been misbehaving?'

'Well, sir, we know Harry Hooper was supposed to be having an affair with the female lead.'

'Nothing secret about that. Hooper probably has it away with all his female leads.'

'Perk of the job you mean?'

'A requisite more like. Look at Warren Beatty and the women he's been forced to go with just because he's a film star. Come on. We'll take Hooper first anyway.'

Harry Hooper was in the star dressing room when the two detectives knocked on his door. He didn't look pleased at being interrupted in the middle of applying his make-up.

He wore his Alice the Cook dress with the padded bosoms, yellow curly wig and multicoloured leggings.

'I've already told your sergeant here where I was on Tuesday morning,' he grumbled to Glass whilst grimly forcing a smile to keep up his public image.

'In your bed without the pleasure of Mrs. Hooper's company I believe?'

The comedian looked up sharply. 'What's that supposed to mean?'

'Nothing,' replied Glass innocently. 'Your good lady, I am told, is residing with her sister in Tunbridge Wells. Is that just for the duration of this pantomime, sir?'

'You know damn well it isn't. She's left me as everybody in the country is well aware. It's been in all the tabloids.'

'I'm afraid I take the Financial Times,' murmured the Inspector, 'and there was no mention of it in there. And I don't think Sergeant Moon spotted it in the Poultry Keepers' Gazette, did you sergeant?'

Before Moon could reply, Glass quickly continued. 'You now live alone then, Mr. Hooper?'

'Most of the time.' His face broke into a smile. 'You're a man of the world, Inspector . . . '

'Chief Inspector.' Glass did not contradict the first half of the sentence.

'I have had the odd er — companion stay from time to time, if you catch my meaning.' Observing the comedian's current attire, Glass wondered at his chances of success in this sphere.

'It's a pity you didn't have a companion on Monday night. She could have confirmed your story. Let me see now,' he consulted a dog-eared notebook, 'you say you slept right through until twelve o'clock, two hours after poor Mr. Cadamarteri was savagely murdered. Do you live far from Mr. Cadamarteri's flat sir?'

'I don't know where his flat is.'

'Chelsea.'

'I live in Hampstead. A good half hour's journey which ever way you travel.'

'So you'd have had to have left your own place at half past nine at the latest?'

'To do what?'

'Slash Mr. Cadamarteri's throat,' said Glass pleasantly.

Harry Hooper threw back his head and gave a throaty laugh that was familiar to millions through his television show. 'Come now, Chief Inspector. I'm a millionaire, I'm the most bankable comedian in the country, why would I risk everything to kill a man whom I hardly know and whose chief claim to fame seems to be playing as the ass-end of a pantomime cow?'

Hooper stood up and stretched to his full six feet. Glass thought he could see the marks on his neck where he'd had the skin tucks but he had to admit the man looked fit for someone in his late fifties, especially if the rumours about his lifestyle were even half true.

'Any number of reasons.' Although the detective couldn't think of a significant one at that precise moment. 'Is there anyone else in the cast who might have had a better reason to kill him?'

'I can't see it. We hardly knew the fellow. He was in his costume most of the time along with his chum, the other old queen. God knows what they were getting up to in there.' He guffawed lasciviously. 'Imagine, all those little kiddies on the front row giggling away at this loveable cow hopping around the stage and all the time the two occupants are stuck up one another enjoying sodomitic orgasms.' Hooper swayed with mirth at the mental picture he had created. Sergeant Moon looked on as if in shock.

'I don't think two of them could be stuck up one another,' pointed out Glass practically. 'They'd probably need at least six of them to form a continuous circle. I believe they call it a daisy chain.'

'Oh, wonderful.' Tears ran down Hooper's cheeks, smudging the red rouge blotches. 'I like it. Ring a ring of roses eh?'

'Did anyone see you leave the flat at twelve?' Glass snapped. The question caught the comedian unawares. He wiped his eyes slowly before answering.

'I didn't leave the flat at twelve. I rose at twelve. I didn't go out until one when I walked to my local for a bar snack and a pint of beer. The barman will confirm it. Just ask for Jamie.'

'Take a note of the address, sergeant. Thank you for your time, Mr. Hooper. We'll be in touch if we need anything further.'

'You can't seriously think he did it,' said Moon as they made their way down the corridor.

'I wish he had. I don't like him, the arrogant sod, but no, I can't see a motive. Let's try Marsha Flint.'

The leading lady of the show had a dressing

room half the size of Harry Hooper's. The walls were papered with good luck telegrams and cards and a cluster of fluffy toys adorned the ledge that served as a dressing table.

Marsha Flint was tiny with a bob of black hair that framed her pale face. She was in her Jack costume, frilled open-neck shirt, tight leggings and thigh high boots, a far cry from the skimpy see-through chiffon bra and PVC mini-skirt that she wore on Top of the Pops.

She also looked a lot older than when she appeared as a schoolgirl in the Australian soap series although that had been only twelve months ago.

'Sorry to disturb you Miss,' smiled Glass, entering before she'd had time to answer his knock and proffering his warrant card. 'Just a few questions about Mr. Cadamarteri.'

'Come on in. I've been expecting you.'

'Really? Why is that?'

'Well, no reason really, I suppose. She giggled. 'But you haven't caught anybody yet have you? so I guessed you'd be doing the rounds again.'

'Did you know Mr. Cadamarteri well?'

'Not really. I didn't have too much to do with him. He seemed a pleasant kind of man, him and his friend, Mr. Oliver.'

'You knew they were gay, of course?'

111

She looked surprised at the question. 'How does that affect anything?'

'Well in this country, there are some people who find homosexuality offensive.' Moon noticed that his superior spoke slowly as if addressing someone who was not familiar with the language. Did he think Australian was a foreign tongue? 'Queer-bashers we call them. I'm not sure of the Antipodean equivalent.'

'I'm hardly a queer basher, Mr. Glass. I'm a lesbian.'

Glass was taken aback. It wasn't the sort of confession women of his acquaintance were apt to come out with so readily. But he recovered his poise quickly.

'So the scurrilous rumours about you and Harry Hooper are untrue?'

'What rumours?'

'That there's something going on between the two of you.'

Marsha Flint threw her head back and laughed in genuine amusement. 'You must be joking. I'd rather shag a cabbage.'

Glass pondered on the feasibility of this and shook his head. He wasn't in tune with the modern woman and such outspokenness from a young girl was anathema to him. It reinforced his decision to stick to women of pensionable age. His widowed friend, Mrs.

Lewthwaite would never have ventured such a sentiment.

'But if you're looking for queer-bashers then try Jim Smith.'

'Who's he?'

Moon intervened. 'He plays The Wicked Baron.'

'And he doesn't like queers?'

'Hates them,' said Marsha. 'He refers to me as 'that dyke' and he was always making nasty comments about the poor old guys in the cow.'

Glass thought. Was homophobia enough of a motive for murder? And, if so, did that mean Marsha was in danger too?

'So you think he might have killed Mr. Cadamarteri because he was gay?'

'No. I said he hated queers. I didn't say he'd kill them. For God's sake, they were harmless enough. They liked a gossip, of course, but nothing malicious. Like a couple of old women really.'

Glass retreated to his planned line of questioning. 'According to your statement, you were in bed at the time Mr. Cadamarteri was murdered?'

'Yes, and all alone, I'm afraid. But I'd no reason to kill the poor man.'

'Do you know anyone who did have a reason?'

'No, but you'd better hurry and find one before poor Mr. Gregory goes the same way.'

'What are you talking about?'

'You mean you haven't heard about last night's accident?' Obviously, judging by their expressions, neither of the detectives had. She leaned closer to them and Glass caught a lungful of Calvin Klein B unisex perfume. 'Oh yes, a piece of scenery fell on top of the pantomime cow. Nearly crushed the bloke in the front half. Luckily for Gregory, he was in the back.'

'Why do you think it was meant for Mr. Oliver? Surely it could have been an accident?'

Marsha shrugged her shoulders. 'Please yourself.'

'Can you tell me any reason why Mr. Oliver should be in any danger.'

'Of course not. Maybe we're all in danger.' She threw her head back dramatically. 'Perhaps there's a madman somewhere in the theatre who doesn't like pantomimes and he's out to kill us all. Maybe someone in a rival company doing badly with their *Cinderella*.' She laughed but Glass wasn't amused.

'If you think of anything else, get in touch with us, please.'

Detective Sergeant Moon closed the door behind them. 'What do you make of that?' he asked.

'I think she just likes to say things for effect but we'll see how Mr. Oliver himself regards the incident.'

They reached the dressing room that had been occupied by the two occupants of the pantomime cow and Glass knocked sharply on the door.

'Come in,' cried a wavery voice and the two men entered. Gregory Oliver was seated at the ledge, dressed in a pair of beige cavalry twill slacks and a blue silk shirt that was unfastened. A few stray grey hairs poked through the white Aertex vest beneath. 'Oh, it's you again, Chief Inspector. I'm afraid I'm feeling a little fragile this evening.'

'I believe you had rather a shock last night, sir.'

'They said it was an accident. A rope came loose or something.'

'Sounds feasible,' said Glass who knew nothing whatsoever about the backstage operations of a theatre.

'I suppose I'd have thought nothing of it if it hadn't been for the car.'

'What car?' Both men were suddenly alert. Gregory explained about his narrow escape on the pavements of Chelsea, how this

115

wonderful dusky lady swung him off his feet to safety as a huge car missed him by inches before roaring off down the street.

When he'd finished the story he waited for the inspector's reaction. It wasn't favourable.

'Imagination. Pure coincidence. Why should anyone want to kill you? What have you done?'

'Nothing. But neither had Maxie and look what happened to him.'

Glass stopped to consider this. What about the queer basher, the Wicked Baron? Surely he'd not taken it upon himself to rid the capital of it's gay population single-handed. He'd have a job, thought Glass. There were more of the buggers every time you looked. Or should it be buggerers.

He gave up pondering semantics and looked hard at the actor. 'You definitely swear that you know of no reason why anyone might want Mr. Cadamateri or yourself out of the way. You've not upset anyone, left a Chinese restaurant without paying . . . ?

Gregory stood up, a slight figure, looking nearer seventy than sixty. 'You're right, of course. I'm getting paranoid. Losing Maxie has upset me. I'm leaving the show after tomorrow' night's performance. I don't think I shall perform again. Retirement beckons.'

116

'The rest will do you good,' said Glass, patronisingly.

'Not without Maxie, it won't. We were going to do so much together.' He started to sob and the detectives quietly took their leave.

'Do you think someone could be trying to kill him?' asked Moon as they returned to the police car.

'I can't see it but I'm not always right,' he replied, in a voice that suggested he was.

Meanwhile, a hundred and fifty miles up North, another young girl was reported missing and the hunt was stepped up for the man they called The Spa Killer.

12

Colin Vickers sold sanitary towels and tampons for a living. The products were not such that afforded him much dignity amongst his acquaintances, most of whom made ribald comments when they discovered his secret. Whenever strangers asked about his job, he would tell them he was a sales representative 'in the hygiene business'.

Vickers was thirty-seven. He lived in a small terraced house in Stratford on Avon with his elderly mother, who was under the impression he dealt in medical supplies. As her age precluded her taking advantage of any possible free samples, the deception didn't harm her.

He worked for a division of a multi-national operation whose headquarters were based in Leeds. His own territory, quaintly described by his company as The Midlands, stretched from London up to Newcastle on Tyne.

There were two other salespersons in the team, another man, who covered Scotland, Ireland and the Isle of Man ('The North'), and a lady from Brighton who worked everywhere below London, 'The South', including the Isle of Wight.

Vickers was a man of unprepossessing appearance. His parting grew wider month by month, ineffectively disguised by combing the thinning strands across his bald pate; his moustache, which he thought gave him the bravura air of a Mexican playboy, made him look like a fat version of Hitler and he had halitosis, not the happiest of conditions for a person in his profession.

He'd got the job because he was a good talker and he did well in it because he was also a good listener. Someone had once described him as 'a man who lived on his wits' and Vickers wouldn't have taken it as an insult.

His love life was less satisfactory. He had had a platonic girlfriend called Glenys on and off for twelve years but, tired of waiting for an engagement ring that never materialised, Glenys sensibly ran off with a Turkish Cypriot waiter whom she met at a late night fast food wagon in Birmingham. Since then there had been no one.

Being frightened of real women, Vickers was forced to satisfy his frequent sexual urges with pornographic films and visits to unpleasant sites on the Internet, combined with the dextrous use of his right wrist, which received enough practice for him to consider an alternative career as a spin bowler for Warwickshire.

Sometimes he thought he'd like to act in these films. He'd seen adverts in various magazines asking for models, but he hesitated about replying in case his mother found out.

At least he'd get to meet girls that way.

On the other hand, he'd recently discovered that the Internet was an interactive medium that allowed him to communicate direct with 'models' who would talk dirty to him and oblige his harmless fantasies in exchange for his credit card number.

Many years ago, he had been found guilty of stealing ladies underwear from washing lines and the resultant court case had frightened him enough to preclude him from overstepping the law again.

In the privacy of his own room, however, he could do what he liked, although it did not stop him from wanting to experience the real thing.

On the afternoon that Detective Chief Inspector Glass was suffering a surfeit of porn in the cinema and Detective Chief Inspector Knox was questioning Judy Whay's school chums in Bath, Colin Vickers was enjoying a cup of tea at the buffet on Stoke-on-Trent station.

He'd had an unsuccessful day. The buyer at the local health authority had proved to be more interested in incontinence pads for his nursing homes rather than any of Colin's products.

He had more calls in the area on the following day so he'd booked to stay the night in a local hotel, the Post House at Newcastle under Lyme.

He parked his company car opposite reception and checked in.

Later, he planned to drive into Henley and buy a paper to see what entertainment was on in town. Maybe a cinema, perhaps a disco or possibly a massage parlour. Had there been licensed brothels, there would have been no dilemma but, as the red light districts of The Potteries offered little of the promise of Amsterdam or Copenhagen, his choices were limited.

One thing was certain. He certainly didn't fancy a lonely evening in his hotel room.

★ ★ ★

On the other side of town, a young girl was coming out of school with her friends. Marian Lynch was fifteen and a bright child. She played clarinet in the school orchestra, was captain of the netball team and was

121

expected to follow in her father's footsteps and become a doctor. Her mother taught an information technology course at the local university.

Which is not to say Marian was a swot. Far from it. She was popular with her classmates, loved The Spice Girls and All Saints, liked going to discos and had a boyfriend, Mark, whom she'd been dating for over a year, although they hadn't slept together.

That night, she and Mark had planned to go to the cinema in Hanley to see the latest Tom Cruise film.

Mark called for her at seven in his lilac painted Volkswagen Beetle, a present from his parents for his recent seventeenth birthday.

'She's not come home from school yet,' Marian's mother told him. 'We're a bit worried.'

They were a lot more worried when there was still no sign of her at ten o'clock. By then, Mrs. Lynch had rung round her daughter's friends and they all confirmed they hadn't seen her since classes ended at three thirty.

Marian had told them she was going to the shops in town to buy some make-up to wear that evening and that was the last sighting they had of her.

By midnight, a police search was underway. All the late night pubs, clubs and discos were checked but of Marian Lynch there was no trace.

★ ★ ★

She was in Boots in Henley comparing colours of lipsticks when Marian met the man who called himself Julian Swift.

He told her he was working for a market research firm and asked her if she could spare five minutes to answer some questions about make-up.

As he was carrying a clipboard, Marian accepted his story.

Julian was tall and good-looking with short brown hair and a shy smile. He wore a charcoal suit with a fashionably loud tie and a pair of shiny black Ikon boots covered his feet. Marian put his age at around twenty. She was four years out.

They went to a pub where she allowed him to buy her a WKD, the alcoholic version of Irn-bru. They took a seat near the bar and he explained that his work as a market researcher also involved him in finding girls who might be suitable to embark upon a career in modelling.

By a great coincidence, Marian was a

girl who seemed to have just the qualities needed.

It could well be, he told her, that if he put her name forward, his company might well be able to offer her work. Part-time at first, of course, but very well paid and who knew what it might lead to. Why, didn't Claudia Schiffer start just like this?

The teenager hadn't a clue how Claudia Schiffer had started but she was quite prepared to accept that she, Marian Lynch, could soon be on the catwalks herself.

They had another drink and Julian brought out his portfolio of models already with the agency. She glanced through the pages. Most of the girls were of a similar age to her and, she thought, no more attractive than she was.

In some of the later shots, the girls were wearing bikinis and underwear but nothing more revealing than you saw in newspaper adverts nowadays.

'I just need a couple of photos of you to put forward to my bosses,' he said. 'Perhaps we could do them now if you've got ten minutes. The studio's only a couple of streets away.'

Marian thought. It was four thirty. Her parents wouldn't be home for another hour. It was an opportunity too good to miss. She agreed to go.

'We'll just have a quick one before we go. Same again?' She nodded. She was already starting to feel a little light-headed. Apart from a bag of salted crisps, she hadn't eaten since breakfast.

One of the barmen came to clear the glasses and gave Marian a suspicious look. She realised she was in her school clothes but he wouldn't know she wasn't in the sixth form so she gave him her most seductive smile and he blushed and walked away. He couldn't have been much more than eighteen himself, she thought.

Julian returned soon afterwards with their third drinks and he proceeded to entertain her with witty conversation and gossip whilst they drank them, before suggesting they make a move.

The pub was in the town centre and was starting to fill up with late afternoon shoppers needing to quench their thirst and shop and office workers finishing the early shift.

As they threaded their way through the crowd clustered round the bar, Marian stumbled and fell against a man carrying a pint of bitter to a vacant table. His glass fell to the floor, spilling beer everywhere.

'I'm sorry,' she gasped.

'That's all right.' The man was almost middle-aged with receding hair and a strangely shaped moustache but his voice was friendly enough. They both stooped to pick up pieces of the shattered glass and Marian's front door key fell out of her school blouse pocket.

The stranger picked it up and handed it back. 'You don't want to lose that.'

She smiled foolishly. 'No. Look, I'll have to get you another drink.'

He looked down at her as she leaned forward, the blouse gaping open enough for him to see the swell of her young breasts over the cups of her black bra. If only he could have her for one night, thought Colin Vickers, but already the boyfriend was turning back.

At that moment, a young barman came up. 'That's all right, you leave it. I'll sweep it up.' As he went for a brush, he looked at Vickers and wondered how old men like that could pull young girls.

'Are you sure I can't give you something,' Marian offered again. Colin Vickers thought there was plenty she could give him but he had no time to reply.

'Something the matter?' The look in the boyfriend's eyes told Vickers there had better not be.

'I knocked his drink over,' gasped Marian.

'It's OK, don't worry about it.' Colin

126

didn't want any trouble.

'You heard what the man said, let's go.' Without another word, Julian led the girl into the street.

'We'll take the car, it's just across the road.' He led her to a blue vehicle parked on double yellow lines and ushered her into the front seat.

By now, Marian Lynch was feeling a tiny bit nervous. The third drink had all but scrambled her brain now the mishap in the pub had unnerved her. And here she was in a car with a complete stranger who could be taking her anywhere.

He took her, in fact, to a lock-up unit on a deserted business park on the edge of town. Marian could see no sign or name anywhere on the building as he unlocked the door and ushered her inside.

The unit was actually let on a five-year tenancy to a company called Monroe Studios, which was another name for Julian Swift although, for some reason, his name did not appear on any of the documents.

Most of the photographic and film work done there was for out of town advertising agencies, which meant there were very few visitors to the premises, a situation that suited the owner.

When he switched on the light, Marian

could see they were in a large film studio with floodlights and various photographic paraphernalia and, because it looked official, she relaxed.

Julian went into a side office and emerged holding a tiny gold bikini. 'Here, put this on.' Marian took the garment from him uncertainly. 'You can change in there while I set up the lights.'

It was only a small office, containing a sofa, a metal filing cabinet, a couple of chairs and an old oak desk on which stood a telephone, a number of envelopes and a calculator.

She wasn't too happy about removing her clothes with a stranger there but, as he had hardly glanced at her when he handed her the bikini, she supposed it would be all right. After all, it was business.

She left her school blouse and skirt in a heap on the sofa along with her underwear and stepped into the studio wearing the skimpy swimwear, just in time to see Julian Swift turning a key in the front door and suddenly Marian Lynch was very afraid.

13

News of Marian Lynch's disappearance greeted Detective Chief Inspector Knox when he reached his desk at Scotland Yard at 7 a.m. the following morning.

'You think it could be him again, sir? The Spa Killer?' asked Detective Sergeant Evans.

'Could be. Could be she'll turn up unharmed but we can't afford to take chances so, for the time being, we'll assume the worst. I want a print-out of all blue Ford Mondeos registered in the Bath area and in The Potteries and then a check through their owners for any sexual offenders.'

'Right.'

'We'll drive up to Stoke this afternoon. In the meantime, get her description circulated. Make sure the people up there have circulated her photo to all the media.'

'No idea who we're looking for, sir?'

Robin thought of his conversation with Otis Ellis. 'A man of about forty, possibly working in the area temporarily and he could have a record for indecent assault or something of that nature.'

129

Sergeant Evans seemed impressed but Knox knew it was needle in a haystack time and time was something they might not have. Judy Whay had died two days after she went missing. The next forty-eight hours could prove vital.

★ ★ ★

In another part of the building, Detective Chief Inspector Glass sat in the canteen with Detective Sergeant Moon, working his way through a cholesterol-packed fry-up washed down with turgid cups of strong canteen tea.

His two main enquiries were not going well and they were both cases he was anxious to solve as quickly as possible.

The 'Pantomime Cow Murder', being show-biz, was very high profile in the press whilst Glass had a personal interest in getting a result in the Himmler Films enquiry after the ruination of his Christmas party, not to mention Sergeant Evans' getting on his back at every turn.

The trouble was, neither investigation seemed to be going anywhere. Nightingale was safely locked up but, as yet, there were no clues to the men who ran Himmler Films.

Similarly, nothing had been found to link

any of the pantomime cast to the murder of Max Cadamarteri.

'I think we'll go back to the theatre and check on that falling piece of scenery,' he decided. 'See if any wires or anything were cut.'

'We'll have to hurry then, there's a matinee on this afternoon.'

But when they arrived, there was nothing to see. It turned out that the errant prop had fallen from a ledge high up in the flies which meant anyone could have climbed up and pushed it without leaving any trace.

'Who was on stage at the time?' asked Glass.

'Just the pantomime cow, two villagers and Jack,' replied the ASM, a hesitant youth in his early twenties who had offered to escort the officers round the theatre and try to answer any questions.

He had a nervous twitch that seemed to be set off whenever the policeman addressed him. Glass found himself stopping momentarily on the brink of a sentence to see if this would delay the movement but it only ended up with the detective speaking like somebody with an unfortunate speech defect.

'And where would the other actors have been at the moment the scenery fell?'

'Depends. Waiting in the wings if they were due on or perhaps back in the dressing room if their next scene was much later. Nobody kept tabs on them.'

'But if somebody went missing, to climb up to the flies, as you call them, for instance, then presumably somebody would notice their absence?'

'Only if they failed to appear on stage for their lines.'

'So, apart from Marsha Flint and the two no-marks who played the villagers . . .'

'I think they still call them actors,' whispered Moon, 'even though they might not have speaking parts.' Glass ignored him.

'Apart from those three, anybody could have done it, is that what you're saying?'

'I don't know. I suppose so.' He sounded worried as if by this confession he was landing all his colleagues in the dock.

'Hang around and have a word with the cast when they arrive,' instructed Glass to his sergeant. 'See if they noticed any of their number go walkabout at . . .' he raised his eyebrows at the ASM. 'What time did the incident occur?'

'About twenty to ten, I think.' The youth consulted his script. 'Yes, nine forty.'

'You've got that, Moon. Nine forty.'

At that moment, a burly man with a black beard burst through the stage door and made his way along the corridor towards them. Glass recognised him as someone who had appeared in small roles in various television comedy series over the years.

'Afternoon, Dan,' he greeted the ASM. He nodded to the policemen.

'Jim,' acknowledged the ASM.

Glass pricked up his ears. 'Jim Smith isn't it? You play the Wicked Baron.'

'That's right.' The man smiled an expansive smile. 'I don't believe we've met but I have spoken to your sergeant here and I think I convinced him I had a watertight alibi for the time of Cadamarteri's murder.'

Sergeant Moon confirmed it. 'He was in bed with his wife, sir. We have Mr. Smith's statement.'

'I'm Detective Chief Inspector Glass, sir. I'm in charge of this investigation.' His voice took on a serious note. 'I'm told you have an aversion to people of the homosexual persuasion.'

If Glass thought the man was going to deny it, he was mistaken. 'You have been told correctly, Chief Inspector. If we were all queer, the human race would die out in a generation so it can't be normal, can it? End of equation.' Back came the smile.

'How strongly do you feel about it?'

'Ah, I see what you're getting at. Do my opinions give me a reason for killing Mr. Cadamarteri?'

'And do they?'

'Certainly not. I wouldn't risk my neck for one of those limp-wristed beggars. Not worth it. Anyway, you've only got to read my statement to know I couldn't have done it.'

'With respect, Mr. Smith, gentlemen's wives have been known to support their spouses in times of need.'

'What are you suggesting?' This time, the smile was replaced by an angry snarl. Instead, it was Glass who beamed benevolently at the actor.

'Why, nothing at all, sir. Nothing at all. Good-day to you.'

'What now, sir?' asked Moon as they walked to the stage door.

'I'll leave you to check with the cast again, Moon. See if they noticed anyone missing when the scenery dropped. I'll see you back at the Yard at six.'

'Where are you going to?'

'It's my Saturday afternoon off, Sergeant. As is my custom, I shall be at Loftus Road watching Queens Park Rangers carry out their usual act of hari-kari in the Nationwide League.'

134

★ ★ ★

The man heading the Stoke-on-Trent enquiry into the disappearance of Marian Lynch was Chief Superintendent Steve Rimmer.

He was a tall man with a sallow complexion and a lithe movement about him that suggested that he could handle himself in an affray, despite his forty-four years.

By the time Robin Knox and Trevor Evans had driven up from London, Rimmer had already made sure that the schoolgirl's picture was going to be featured in every evening paper that night within a fifty mile radius and on all the television newsreels.

The local radio stations carried a plea for people to get in touch with the police if they had seen the missing girl.

The Superintendent himself had appeared on a lunchtime T.V. interview, along with Marian's parents and boyfriend, appealing to members of the public to come forward if they had any information.

'Any joy so far?' asked Knox after introductions had been effected.

'We've spoken to the parents. The girl had a key to let herself in as they both work. One or other of them usually gets back by six. The father's a doctor at the Health Centre and the mother lectures at University. Both

135

distraught as you can imagine. She's had a rather sheltered upbringing.'

'Boyfriend?'

'Mark Peters. Only seventeen. A nice lad. Comes from a good family. He spent all last night looking for her round the discos and bars in town with his mates.'

'What about her school friends?'

'She left them after classes to go shopping in Henley.'

'And nobody's seen her since?'

'No. But it's early days.

'Early days nothing,' the Chief Inspector reminded him soberly. 'If this case goes the way of the last Spa killing, time is against us. The equivalent of twenty four hours from now, Judy Whay was dead.'

Knox gave him what little information he had on the other victims. It wasn't much. Steve Rimmer shuddered when the nature of the victims' injuries was revealed to him.

'The blue Mondeo is the only real clue we've had so far,' said Knox, 'and that's a longshot at best. We're checking registered owners at the moment.'

'I'll get onto the radio and TV people now and get it in the next bulletin. Someone might have seen it.'

The first real breakthrough came early in the evening. A young man called Matt

Moogan, who worked part-time in a town centre pub, came into police headquarters to say he had seen Marian Lynch the previous afternoon.

'I noticed her because she was in school uniform so I thought she might be under age. To be drinking, like.'

'Why didn't you do anything about it?' asked Superintendent Rimmer with a friendly smile.

The youth stuttered his face a bright red. 'Well, I wasn't sure. I mean, she could have been older. Anyway, she was with this bloke.'

'Ah.' This was the important bit. 'Can you give us a description of him?'

'He was about forty five, no maybe not that old, forty.'

'How tall was he?'

'I don't know. About my height I think. Average.' Moogan was five foot eight.

'Was he fat? Did he have any distinguishing marks?'

'Plumpish, I suppose. He had a moustache. He looked seedy.'

'What colour hair?'

'Brownish.'

'Long?'

Matt Moogan thought long and hard. 'Longish,' he said at last.

'What was he wearing?'

'A suit, I think. I noticed his tie. Very loud, lots of colours.'

Knox sighed. It was hardly a definitive portrait but it was better than nothing.

'You didn't see them leave?'

''Fraid not.'

He was taken to complete an identikit likeness on the computer, which would be circulated by wire to every police station and newspaper in Britain by midnight.

'What do you think?' Superintendent Rimmer asked.

Knox looked unsure. 'It's the best lead we've had so far. I mean there's no doubt it's the girl but we could have done with a better description of the bloke with her.'

'The lad may do better when he gets on the computer. Meanwhile, let's hope other people have read the papers. Someone might have seen the girl.'

* * *

One person who had seen Marian Lynch's photograph in the evening papers was Colin Vickers.

He had had a delivery to make in Longton on Saturday morning, which kept him in the area. After completing his task, he drove

138

across to Henley to look round the shops. Late in the afternoon, he came across a tearoom on the top floor of a curtain shop. Feeling peckish, he ventured up the stairs, ordered a pot of tea and a roast turkey sandwich and took out the early edition of the evening paper he had bought earlier.

Staring at him from the front page, under the headline HAVE YOU SEEN THIS GIRL? was a face he recognised.

Colin had not had an exciting night in Stoke on Trent. The most erotic film he could find in the local cinema was 101 *Dalmatians* and the discos seemed to be full of fifteen-year-old babes who wouldn't look twice at anyone over twenty-five.

In the end, as always, he went back to his hotel with his copy of Fiesta and speculated on whether he should invest in a blow-up woman. With his luck, though, she would probably get a puncture. Difficult to explain at the bicycle repair shop.

In fact, the outstanding event of the day had been his encounter in the late afternoon with the schoolgirl he'd bumped into in the pub. She'd almost fallen out of her blouse when she'd bent down to pick up the key she'd dropped. He hadn't been as close to a lovely pair of tits as those for a long time. He'd managed to climax twice in the hotel room just thinking about them.

What a shock it was, therefore, to see the girl's face staring out at him now from the front page of the Evening Sentinel.

When he realised she was missing he went cold. What if anyone had seen him in the pub talking to her? He was very aware of his criminal record. If anyone in the pub had seen him and told the police, they might think he'd abducted her.

Then common sense took a hold. He was in a strange town, miles from where he lived in Stratford on Avon. Nobody in a crowded Henley pub would have known him.

Would they?

He looked at his watch. He had better leave town quickly. He was about to jump up when the waitress brought his meal. Avoiding her glance, he sat down again and began to stuff the sandwiches furiously into his mouth.

Ten minutes later, he was back in the car park. He started the engine of his blue Ford Mondeo and headed for the southbound M6 towards Stratford and home.

14

Gregory Oliver got through the matinee performance of *Jack and the Beanstalk* without mishap. This time he played the front half of the cow, which allowed him to stand upright, and a lady called Diana was recruited from the chorus line to join him at the hip, as it were, to form the animal's rear.

As there was only a two hour gap between the end of the matinee and the start of the evening show, most of the cast usually stayed on the premises and brought along some food and drink to sustain them for the late performance.

However, to mark Gregory's last night, and as a belated tribute to his erstwhile partner, the late Max Cadamarteri, Marsha Flint had organised a party. A catering company delivered a finger buffet, a local pub sent along bottles of imitation champagne and Marsha had organised a giant iced cake with the inscription 'To Max and Gregory — a great team'.

Gregory was quite overcome at the gesture and when the assembled thespians joined in to sing 'For he's a jolly good fellow'; he couldn't hold back the tears.

Sergeant Moon, who was present at the celebrations, was also suitably moved.

'The old fellow couldn't speak,' he told his superior later. 'He was so upset.'

Glass glared at him. He was equally upset. Not only had the sergeant failed to elicit any more information from his latest enquiries, but also Queens Park Rangers had sustained another defeat making relegation a distinct possibility.

'But he managed to survive the afternoon?' he snarled eventually. 'The beanstalk didn't strangle him?'

'You don't go for the attempted murder theory then?' said Moon.

'I'd like to. A motive for killing both of them might be easier to find than a motive for killing one but I can't honestly see it. Coincidence that's all. People read too much into things.'

'Mmmmm.' Moon thought it wiser not to come down on either side in case he chose the wrong one. 'We're still looking for the weapon,' he added. 'Perhaps that will tell us something.'

'Doubt if we'll find it,' said his Chief Inspector. 'But we'll stick around the theatre for a while. Someone will say something.' He checked the battered chronograph on his left wrist. 'In fact, the evening performance will be just starting. I'd like to be there to see Mr. Oliver's final bow; that is if he isn't too sloshed on cheap bubbly to put one hoof in front of the other.'

Sergeant Moon groaned. He didn't think he could stand another three hours of Jack and the Beanstalk but, as luck would have it, he didn't have to. Just as they were about to leave, the message came through from Wormwood Scrubs.

Gordon Nightingale had hung himself in his cell.

★ ★ ★

Detective Chief Inspector Glass was on the scene within the hour. Nightingale's body was still *in situ*, paramedics having done all they could to revive him but without success.

A vivid collar of blood stood out on his neck where the wire had cut into the flesh.

'Best thing that could have happened to him,' mused Glass philosophically. 'Gives him the chance to make a fresh start somewhere else.' He wondered if his action in mentioning Gordon Nightingale's name at the Soho Sex Emporium had perhaps precipitated the youth's death.

The prison officer didn't seem impressed by the detective's faith in the hereafter. 'There's going to be big trouble over this,' he said. 'Heads will roll. A government enquiry I shouldn't wonder.'

'Quite right, too. Christ, you had the bugger under lock and key and you still can't stop him from escaping,' Glass gave a sarcastic cough, 'albeit to the next world. You're not fit to run a brothel in a monastery. I wonder you didn't hand him the rope.'

'It was a length of wire that he used and, from what we can gather, it was smuggled in by a visitor.'

'Who was the visitor?' asked the detective, interested.

'She gave her name as Lancaster but the address she gave turned out to be spurious.'

'You don't say. What a surprise! I take it there is a picture on a security video somewhere in the building?'

'We have someone checking the film as we speak.'

'I'll hang on till you get them. Someone was afraid that Gordon Nightingale knew more than he admitted and I want to know who that someone was.'

★ ★ ★

144

When Julian Swift turned the key in the lock of the deserted film studio, he could see his action had alarmed the young schoolgirl but he wasn't too worried. Any minute now, he knew the effects of the Roofie that he had slipped into her last drink, would start to take effect.

Within two hours, with 2mg of Rohypnol inside her system, Marian Lynch would be acquiescent to anything Julian Swift might suggest, however repugnant she might have found his actions in normal circumstances.

Furthermore, Flunitrazepam, to give it its generic name, had the additional attribute of impairing the memory, which was why, in America, it had become known as the 'date rape' drug.

'Are you ready,' smiled Julian, turning towards her and slipping the key into his pocket.

'Why did you lock the door?' she stammered.

'There's been some vandalism on the estate lately. We don't want any yobboes barging in, do we?' He put his arm round her reassuringly. 'You know, you look beautiful in that bikini.'

She smiled back at him. She was being nervous over nothing. Obviously no harm was going to come to her and she remembered again his words about a modelling career.

Julian went into the office and brought out a camera and flash. 'Are you ready?'

She nodded. 'How do you want me?' She was beginning to feel, not sleepy but somehow relaxed and out of control. As if she'd had a few drinks too many but she'd only had three.

When Julian suggested she remove the top half of the bikini, she didn't hesitate for a moment. Later, the rest of it came off and she posed for pictures that would have befitted an advanced manual of gynaecology.

'I'll just set up the video,' Julian said at last, having used four rolls of film, 'and we'll try a movie.'

Marian thought that sounded a good idea. A warm, sensual feeling had overtaken her as she watched Julian put the camera and lights in place and set the motor running.

'Right,' he said. 'You're going to be a film star.' He began to remove his clothes. 'Are you still a virgin?'

Marian confessed she was.

'Then this is going to be a special production. The deflowering of a beautiful young schoolgirl. It can only happen once.'

Marian felt she ought to protest. She was under sixteen. Her parents would be horrified. She might get pregnant. She might catch AIDS. She'd only just met this boy . . .

But none of it seemed to matter. She felt her body reaches out to him as, naked, he moved towards her and proceeded to spend the next hour abusing her body in ways most women are fortunate never to experience even in their wildest nightmares. Thankfully, the anaesthetic properties of the Roofie spared Marian most of the pain.

By the time Swift was through, Marian was unconscious. Quickly, her antagonist dressed himself then spent ten minutes storing away the film equipment. The videotape of their union he carefully placed in a special padded envelope to take away with him.

Going into the office, Swift collected all Marian's clothes and thrust them into a sports holdall. He couldn't be bothered to dress her. It was dark outside so nobody would see her. He took an old coat that was lying on a sofa and took that to drape round her unclothed body.

Slowly, he opened the front door and peered outside. Everything was still. He could see nobody in sight. He unlocked the car with the remote control and went back to fetch the girl, carrying her out like a giant rag doll.

He leant her against the car whilst he opened the rear door then he dragged her onto the back seat and propped her up against the window, securing her with the seat belt. She was still unconscious and her breathing was shallow. He hoped he hadn't given her too big a dose. There was a lot of work to do with her yet. He'd received his instructions.

He returned to collect the video and to make a last check that he'd left nothing behind. Finally, he locked the studio door after him before climbing into the driver's seat. He looked at his watch. It was eight thirty.

He started the engine and turned the blue car in the direction of the southbound M6 motorway.

The first step of his mission had been completed.

But Julian Swift had made two big mistakes.

* * *

When Marian Lynch had undressed in the office earlier in the afternoon, her front door key had been in the pocket of her school blouse but when Swift roughly gathered her clothes together later, it fell out and it now lay on the floor of the office underneath the oak desk.

Mistake number one.

Mistake number two was potentially more dangerous. The presence of an unseen witness.

Whilst Swift and the girl were inside the studio, a nineteen year old youth named Willy Burr was waiting to burgle the premises of a computer software company called Pritchard Peripherals across the road.

Willy had driven into the business park ten minutes earlier but he had seen Swift's car outside his studio so he drove his Suzuki Vitara further down the road until he turned a corner out of sight of Swift's lock-up. Then he walked surreptitiously back, under the cover of a sparse row of bushes, to watch out for the driver leaving.

He was somewhat surprised to see the man carrying to his vehicle what looked like a lifeless body, which he put on the back seat of his car.

However, the young burglar decided this was none of his business and set about the task in hand which was the removal of several items of value from Pritchards Peripherals' building.

Willy had cased the joint some days earlier and had decided that his best plan would be to gain entry through a window round the back.

Being a novice at the game and not of the

highest intelligence, Willy failed to take into account the fact that Pritchards, a company in the forefront of information technology, naturally employed a state of the art security system. Thus, at the very moment the youth was climbing through the window, an alarm was activated at police headquarters less than two miles away.

Unfortunately for Willy, the alarm didn't sound on the actual premises which is why he was unpleasantly surprised to see a patrol car roar up to the building and two uniformed policemen jump out just as he was emerging with an armful of booty.

The taller and older of the two officers greeted him like an old friend. 'Well well! if it isn't Willy Burr. Fancy seeing you here.'

'Sod you, Rinstead.'

'Going in for big time crime now, are we?' grinned P.C. Rinstead. 'Had enough of snatching handbags from old ladies?' He reached for the youth's arm and his colleague quickly grabbed hold of the boxes of software before they fell to the ground. 'Right. Get moving, son.'

Constable Rinstead pushed his prisoner forward but Willy stood his ground.

'Hang on a minute, what about my ca . . .' He stopped suddenly as he remembered that there was no tax disc on the Vitara.

The constable grinned. 'Don't worry. We'll get the traffic boys to pick it up for you then they can add their charges to our breaking and entering one. Let's go.' And he frog-marched the hapless youth towards the police Escort.

'Piss off, you bastard. Big time for you, is it, catching small time fellows like me instead of going after real criminals?'

'Oh, you're big time, Willy. Normally we deal with litter louts and people cycling on the pavement, don't we John?'

P.C. John Adams grunted.

'Tell you what.' A cunning grin appeared on Willy's face. 'What if I can give you some information about a murder? Can we do a deal?'

Constable Rinstead twisted the youths arm up to his shoulder. 'Withholding information will get you a broken wrist, son. If you know something, you'd better talk.' He gave the limb an extra jerk. 'And quickly, otherwise . . .'

'All right, I'll tell you. Let me go.'

They reached the car and the two policemen allowed Willy to lean against the side of it whilst he told them about the stranger carrying the body out of the lock-up down the road.

'And you're sure it was a body?' asked

151

Rinstead when he'd finished his story.

'Yeah.'

'What about the car?'

'What about it?'

'What make was it?' persisted the policeman patiently.

'A Ford, I think. Yeah, a Ford. A blue one. Don't ask me what sort.'

'What do you think?' asked the other constable.

P.C. Rinstead pursed his lips. 'I suppose we should report it. Just in case.'

Adams gave Willy a push in the chest. 'You'd better not be having us on, sunshine.' He was not much older than the youth but stockily built and with a nasty temper.

'I'll get on to H.Q.'

Chief Superintendent Steve Rimmer happened to be in the control room when the call was radioed through.

'Man seen loading what looked like a body into a blue vehicle at the Business Park,' volunteered the radio operator. 'Did you say a blue car?' snapped Rimmer.

'Yes sir,' confirmed the radio operator. 'A blue Ford.'

'What do you think?' the Superintendent asked Detective Chief Inspector Knox who was standing beside him. 'It's an outside chance but . . .'

'We've got to go for it,' said Robin Knox. 'That Mondeo's our only lead.'

'You're right. Tell all motorway patrols,' he instructed the radio operator, 'to check the plates of every blue Ford they see in the next hour. This could be the break-through we're looking for.'

Superintendent Rimmer was right. It could have been the break-through they were looking for, except for the fact that Willy Burr was no expert on cars, Julian Swift's vehicle was actually a Toyota Carina, whilst Colin Vickers' blue Ford Mondeo was safely in it's Stratford on Avon garage by the time the call went out.

By which time, Marian Lynch was well on her way to her next destination.

15

Sunday morning at the Knox household was somewhat subdued. Robin had not come home at all the previous evening. He was still in Stoke, tied up with the missing schoolgirl enquiry.

There was a possibility the incident was connected with the Judy Whay case that he was already investigating and the word at the Yard was that Marian Lynch might be in danger of becoming the fourth victim of the so-called Spa Killer.

Sue's father had not reached his bed until 2 a.m., having been called to inspect the body of Gordon Nightingale found hanging in his prison cell.

'You should have seen it,' he told his daughter enthusiastically, as he tucked into a hearty breakfast. 'Lumps of skin hanging from his neck where the wire had cut through, dripping with blood and his tongue sticking out of his bloated lips like a pig in a slaughterhouse. Is there any more fried bread?' He scraped the remains of fried egg and black pudding from his plate with a knife and licked the edge dangerously.

154

'No, there isn't.' Sue swallowed hard. This was just what she needed first thing in the day to accompany her morning sickness. 'You'll have to make do with toast and marmalade.'

'The wire was smuggled in by a lady visitor. I've seen the pictures from the security camera but they tell us nothing. Personally, I think it was a man in drag.'

'You've been watching too much Lily Savage.'

'I preferred Mrs. Shufflewick.'

'Who's Mrs. Shufflewick?'

'Radio comedian just after the War. I thought everyone had heard of him. His real name was Rex somebody.'

Sue sighed exasperatingly. 'Do you like anybody who's still alive?'

'Alistair Cooke.'

'He must be ninety by now.'

'Still alive though, that was the criteria.'

'The eighties and nineties have passed you by really, haven't they, Dad?'

Glass supposed they had but didn't feel he'd missed anything. 'Any word from Robin?' he asked, spreading thick butter on his toast. Sue and Robin had converted to Olivio.

'Only that he's staying overnight.'

'Oh.' He took a slurp from a mug of strong tea.

'What's happened with your Pantomime Cow case?' Sue was anxious to steer her father away from the gory details of Gordon Nightingale's demise.

'Nothing. Total blank. Never mind. Something will turn up.' Glass was ever the optimist.

'Didn't you say someone was trying to kill the other chap that was in the cow with him?'

'He said they were. I'm not so sure. I think he's a bit paranoid, myself. Now that Harry Hooper, he's the opposite of paranoid.'

'How do you mean?'

'He labours under the delusion that people like him.' Glass chuckled at his little joke.

'And don't they?' queried Sue. 'I think he's very funny on television.'

'Means nothing. Half these comedians in real life are moody buggers or worse. Look at Charlie Chaplin; they're saying now he was a paedophile and Tony Hancock and Kenneth Williams weren't exactly a bundle of laughs off screen. Ended up topping themselves.'

'Oh dear, you're cheerful today, aren't you? I hope Robin's having better luck with his case.'

Her father reached for the Sunday Times

156

and saw the picture of Marian Lynch on the front page. 'Poor kid,' he said, sadly. 'I don't give much for her chances.'

There was also an Identikit picture of a man the police wanted to interview. He looked very like the England football goalkeeper, David Seaman.

The detective turned to his daughter. 'Luck?' he repeated. 'I'm afraid Robin will need all the luck he can get with this one.'

★ ★ ★

Up in the Potteries, Robin Knox was not getting any of the luck at all. The car check had proved a total fiasco. Blue cars were racing up and down the motorway in profusion and the fraction of registration numbers that the patrol car drivers had managed to obtain had all led nowhere.

They had had no better luck with the check of blue Mondeos registered in Bath and the Stoke area. Three of the registered owners had records for sexual offences but one was still in jail, one was dead and the third was on holiday, pursuing his hobby in Bangkok.

'He's given us the slip,' admitted Superintendent Rimmer, who was in the office for seven o'clock, five hours after he had left for the night.

'Never mind,' said Knox. 'Something might turn up in the building. If, of course, that little toe-rag wasn't lying to take attention away from himself.'

They made their way to the Business Park at first light. 'The owner seems to be a J. Smith according to our information, trading as Monroe Studios. We've had no dealings with them before.'

'What's his address?'

'All we have is a key address in case of emergencies but that's turned out to be a multi occupation house in the middle of town where no-one had heard of our Mr. Smith.'

'Reasonably suspicious,' commented Robin.

The Business Park was deserted as the police car turned into the driveway of Julian Swift's lock-up.

'Locked with a Chubb seven lever,' Sergeant Evans informed them after examining the front door lock. 'And bars on the windows. Obviously he thought he had something worth protecting.'

Robin Knox looked at the bars and shuddered. It reminded him of a prison. 'Do we have a search warrant?' he asked.

'Bugger that.' Trevor Evans marched up to

the door and gave it a healthy boot with his size eleven's. The doorjamb splintered open on the fifth kick.

'Let's go,' said Steve Rimmer.

The three officers marched into the building leaving the driver in the car. 'Careful not to touch anything, there may be prints,' warned the Scotland Yard man unnecessarily.

They spent the next half-hour giving the place a thorough search. They checked the photo and film equipment in the studio, found the small toilet and looked in the cistern and even searched inside the fridge, electric kettle and Belling cooker in the tiny kitchenette.

They found nothing to suggest that Marian Lynch had ever been there.

Finally, they repaired to the office and for the next twenty minutes looked through every portfolio, went through all the stationery and read every letter they could find.

'Seems like a genuine business,' said Knox. 'He deals mainly with advertising agencies by the look of it.'

'I've been through the albums,' Sergeant Evans told them, 'but none of the faces in them resemble the missing girl.'

'It was worth a try but it looks like we've drawn a blank,' admitted Superintendent

Rimmer at last. 'No trace of the girl here. I'll get someone down to secure the door.'

As that moment, his mobile phone rang and as he pulled it out of his pocket, a pound coin fell out and rolled under the desk. Robin Knox bent down athletically to pick it up when his eye caught sight of an object lying near the leg of the desk. It was a front door key.

Robin pulled out a handkerchief and, wrapping it round his fingers, took hold of the key and slipped it into one of the envelopes lying on Julian Swift's desk.

'This,' said the Chief Inspector, 'could be important.'

* * *

Gregory Oliver spent most of Sunday morning in bed. He had a hangover from the celebrations the night before which had continued well after the end of the evening performance of *Jack and the Beanstalk*.

He had been greatly touched when the cast had presented him with two momentos of the occasion, a C.D. of Noel Coward's Greatest Hits and a brilliant red brocade dressing gown in the style of The Master.

Eventually, Gregory crawled out of bed and made his way gingerly to the kitchen where he took a large dose of Andrews Liver Salts to relieve the throbbing in his head.

He resolved to stick to real champagne in future.

The depression that overtook him every morning was beginning to descend again as once more he realised that he was now on his own and he wouldn't ever see his beloved Maxie again.

He had spent every day since his partner's death trying to think of a reason for his brutal murder but none came to mind. They had had no secrets from one another, no money worries, no enemies.

Yet somebody had killed Max Cadamarteri.

What was there in his private life, wondered Gregory, that Max hadn't confided in him? One thing he knew, he would never be able to rest until he had found out.

The police had been through all Max's papers but to no avail. Had they though, thought Gregory, managed to discover the secret drawer in Max's old roll-top desk.

He went over to the desk and slid open the top. The compartment in question was cunningly concealed in the upper part of the desk, behind the third drawer from the top, which was a few inches shorter than the others in the row.

Gregory took out the drawer in question

and pressed a spring, which allowed the false back to swing open, revealing the hidden space behind.

Inside, to his amazement, was a bundle of new five-pound notes, a hundred of them in total. He counted them twice to make sure, then laid them down on the desk top. He was puzzled.

Why had Max hidden away five hundred pounds? Gregory sat down on the nearby chaise longue to consider this. Of course, it didn't follow there was some sinister or hidden meaning. Max could have saved up to pay for his funeral, for instance.

Except that neither he or Max ever saved anything. 'Spend today, die tomorrow,' Max used to say. So why had he hidden all this money in the desk? Indeed, where had it come from? Normally, their income was paid into a joint bank account from which they drew cash, as they needed it, mostly from hole in the wall dispensers. A sum this large had not come from that source.

Gregory rose again and went back to the desk to see if he'd missed anything and found he had. A small leather bound book was wedged at the bottom of the compartment. Gregory pulled it out. It was a diary.

'So that's where he kept it,' he thought. He'd long suspected that Max had written a diary but he'd never seen it before. He flicked through the page. There wasn't an entry every day, just a scattering of musings at intervals throughout the book.

Gregory turned to December, hoping to find some clue to his friend's murder but the entries were mundane to say the least. On December 3rd, for example, Max had written . . .

Rehearsals boring as ever. The director spent half the afternoon with a man from the garden centre, auditioning plants to play the beanstalk. I ask you! Gregory was very tiresome today. Why does he always moan about his part? I told him he could have the front of the cow if he wanted. He says being at the back is like playing Quasimodo. Perhaps we should try for Phantom next year.

Gregory smiled to himself and shut the book. As he did so, a scrap of paper fell to the ground. He picked it up and saw it was a drawing of a snake against the background of what looked like a large cigar. Gregory took it over to the window where he was able to make out the forked tongue, the eyes and the mottled body.

There was no writing but he knew that Max had drawn the sketch because of the italic nib used. Max had always prided himself on his Gothic calligraphy.

But what did it mean? Why had Max kept it hidden so carefully inside his diary? Was there any connection with the money? Or with Maxie's death? Should he show it to the police?

Gregory was never a decisive man at the best of times and, after the trauma of his recent bereavement, he wasn't exactly running on a full shoe of spikes.

A ring on his doorbell interrupted his reverie. Gregory quickly picked up the notes and the diary, thrust them back into the desk and closed the lid before going to see who was at the door.

He didn't notice the paper with the snake on it slip to the floor.

'Oh,' he said, opening it. 'This is a surprise.'

'Can I come in for a moment?'

'Of course, I'm sorry.' Gregory stepped aside to let his visitor through, shutting the door after him. 'I was just going to put the kettle on,' he said, turning towards the kitchen. 'Would you care for a cup of . . .'

He never got to finish the sentence. The first blow on his temple probably killed him but then the assailant slit open Gregory Oliver's throat to make absolutely sure that he never spoke again.

16

'The first blow on the temple probably killed him,' said Detective Chief Inspector Glass.

Detective Sergeant Moon agreed. 'He wouldn't have known what hit him.'

'At least he'll be with his friend again.' Glass had always been seduced by the idea of a glamorous after-life. There were times he couldn't wait to get there.

The police had been called to the scene of the crime by a neighbour returning from church who had seen Gregory Oliver's front door open, peered inside and found the entertainer's body slumped in the lounge.

The neighbour was still hanging around when the two Scotland Yard men arrived. He was in his late sixties and wore a beige car coat with imitation leather edging, open to reveal a cable knit grey cardigan, which matched his grey slip-on shoes. A ring of thin silver hair encircled his liver-spotted skull. Glass thought he looked like a Daily Telegraph reader.

'You must be very frightened living here after two murders in a week,' said the policeman sympathetically.

'Bollocks to being frightened,' the pensioner replied. 'Think of the sodding property values in this block now. You won't be able to give these flats away at this rate.'

The police doctor arrived shortly after them. 'Pretty straightforward,' Glass told her. 'Someone clobbered the poor sod on the head then cut his throat.'

'Clever of you to notice, Chief Inspector,' she replied acidly, observing the bloodstained bruise on Gregory's skull. 'I would have had it down for a poisoning.'

Dr. Francesca Moorcock was in her early thirties, an attractive woman with bright red hair and a reputation as a man-eater. Her sarcasm was wasted on Glass.

'And banged his head on the sideboard as he fell, you mean, subsequently cutting his throat on the empty deadly nightshade bottle lying on the floor. An interesting theory.'

Dr. Moorcock set to work and quickly confirmed that it did indeed appear that death had occurred within the last hour as a result of a blow to the head

'No witnesses and no weapon,' bemoaned Glass. 'Hello, what's this?' He picked up a piece of paper that lay beside the body. It had on it the picture of a snake climbing up some sort of tube.

166

DS Moon leaned across to see it. 'I think it's a python.'

'I didn't know you were an authority on reptiles?'

'I'm not, sir. But pythons are pretty common aren't they? A lot of magicians use them nowadays in their stage acts.'

'I believe they're very popular with male strippers too,' said Dr. Moorcock. 'They like to have something to pop out of their G-strings.'

Glass looked skyward. He had never been able to come to terms with the outspokenness of modern women, having been brought up in a generation of fading violets who would reached for the sal volatile at the first sight of a man's naked chest.

The detective put the paper in his pocket. 'I've got a hunch that this could mean something, though God knows what. He said someone was trying to kill him and he was right. All we have to find out, Sergeant, is who and why.'

★ ★ ★

A plain-clothes detective entered the Operations Room at Stoke and handed Superintendent Rimmer a computer print out. 'We've checked the car registration numbers of all the hotel guests in the area this weekend,' he said, 'and we've come up with four blue Mondeos.'

Rimmer glanced at it then passed it to the two Scotland Yard men. 'These names mean anything to you?

'I think we can disregard the woman, at least for the time being. Knox read out the second name. 'Christopher Mills of Church Road, Matlock, 42 years old.'

'Matlock's a spa town, isn't it?' asked Sergeant Evans. 'I wonder if that's significant.'

'Could be. Next one's Steve Maker, 28, lives in Bristol.'

'Bristol is where Judy Whay was last seen, and in a blue Mondeo.'

'So either of those two could be in the frame.'

'The last one is a company car,' said Steve Rimmer. 'Owned by SanDan, the drug and hygiene people. So the guy's obviously repping for them. He's signed the register Colin Vickers of Percy Street, Stratford on Avon.'

'Do we know how old he is?'

'No but I'd say between 20 and 40 wouldn't you. Usual age for salesmen. You don't see many blokes over forty on the road these days.'

'Interesting,' said Knox.

'Is it?'

'Mmmm. You've heard of Otis Ellis, the criminal profiler?'

Rimmer nodded. 'He was in the news over that Brunskill case a couple of months ago. Picked out the chauffeur Blight as a depraved serial killer.'

'That's right. Well . . . ' Robin went on to outline for him Ellis's criteria for potential serial killers. 'Out of the three suspects, this man Vickers looks like he could fit the bill. Do we know anything else about him?'

The plain-clothes man passed across another sheet of paper. 'I've been on to the police in the towns you mentioned, sir, and they've checked the names and addresses on the licences with the local electoral register.'

Steve Rimmer took the paper and studied it. 'According to this, Steve Maker lives on his own but there are four names in the Mills household, Sandra, Joanne and Louise. At a guess I'd say he had a wife and two daughters.'

'What about Vickers?'

'The only other name at this address is Maud Vickers.'

'Got to be his mother,' said Knox, 'nobody born in the last thirty years can have been christened Maud. It's getting better. Has he got a criminal record?'

'We're still checking that, sir,' said the detective.

'We have done a search on blue Mondeo's from this area but this one came from Stratford so, if there was anything against Vickers, it won't have shown up. Radio through to us when you know, would you. We'll be returning to London shortly.'

'Why don't we take the M40 when we go back to town?' suggested Sergeant Evans. 'Then we could stop off at Stratford on the way and look in on this Mr. Vickers.'

'Good idea, Sergeant. We could even stop for a meal at the Arden Hotel.' Knox enjoyed good food and didn't regard eating in Little Chefs as a gourmet experience.

The first call came when they were still on the M6, negotiating heavy traffic near the junction with the M42. It was Scotland Yard, informing them of the death of Gordon Nightingale in custody.

Sergeant Evans took the news stoically. 'In a way, I'm glad he's dead. At least he'll be no danger to anyone else and, let's face it, he would have been out of prison before he was thirty.'

'But?' asked Knox, sensing there was more.

'I don't know. I suppose I would like him to have suffered a bit. Topping yourself's the easy way out, isn't it?' He thought a moment.

'Then again, I think I would have liked to have had a serious talk with him; find out why he was doing it.'

'From what I heard, you were ready to beat the living daylights out of him last time you had the chance.'

'True,' admitted Evans, 'but sometimes I think there may be something in this theory of bringing the criminal face to face with the victim.'

'I wouldn't let Walter Glass hear you say that.'

Trevor Evans laughed. 'I suppose not. But you wonder how much of a deterrent punishment is sometimes.'

'Forget the deterrent element. At least people can't commit other offences whilst they're locked up. That seems a pretty obvious justification for prisons to me.'

The discussion was interrupted by a second call, this time from Superintendent Rimmer. 'We've got the information you wanted. Two of the men on that list have convictions.'

'Double the amount you'd expect.' Knox had been told at Police College that one in four of the adult population is found guilty of transgressing the law at some time in their lives. As a new recruit, he'd found it difficult to accept that such a high percentage of people had criminal records.

'I can't believe one in four people have a record,' he told Detective Chief Inspector Glass at the time. The older man was more cynical. 'When you've done this job as long as I have,' he remarked, 'you'll realise it's because we never catch the other two.'

Steve Rimmer continued. 'Steve Maker has been done twice for drug offences. Small time dealing. He copped a fine first time, then a six-month sentence. Colin Vickers was arrested back in 1979 for stealing ladies underwear from a clothesline. He got probation.'

'That's more like it.' Robin Knox was beaming. 'It's exactly as Otis Ellis predicted,' he told Sergeant Evans. 'A middle aged man, travelling round the country, living with his mother and with a criminal record for a minor sexual offence.'

'Hang on a minute, sir,' cautioned Evans. 'We don't know he's actually done anything yet. After all, stealing a pair of knickers off a clothesline is hardly a sexual offence, is it? He might have just wanted to blow his nose.'

'He's our man, I'd lay my pension on it,' said Robin Knox. They were now on the M40. 'Put the siren on. We can be in Stratford in half an hour if you put your foot down. There's a girl's life at stake here.'

The pity was, he thought, he'd found Colin Vickers a week too late to save Judy Whay.

The sergeant obeyed dutifully but he didn't share his chief's convictions. Somehow it all seemed too easy and if there was one thing Trevor Evans had learnt in the Force it was that things never came easy.

17

After forensic had been and gone and Gregory Oliver was taken away in a body bag, Detective Chief Inspector Glass and Detective Sergeant Moon had another look round the flat, so recently the home of the two ageing thespians.

'That's funny,' commented Glass. 'This wasn't here before.' He was standing beside the open desk and holding a bundle of five-pound notes. 'Must be over five hundred pounds.'

'He must have drawn it out of the bank since last Tuesday. There was nothing on the statements we saw.'

'Mmmm. I wonder. Anyway, we can easily check that tomorrow. Hello. What's this?' He opened up the small black leather book. 'Well, well. Max Cadamarteri's diary.' He flicked through the pages.

'Anything interesting?' enquired Moon.

Glass read out. *Show going wonderfully. I adore 'Figaro' and how marvellous to be doing a proper show at last. Greg and I had a trip out on the bay today. Not Naples but we had a ripping time. Oh, the faded grandeur of the English seaside resorts.* 'That was the July 10th. entry. It's all like that. No revelations that I can see. Here, have a look.'

The sergeant spent a few minutes reading the later entries then shook his head. 'Nothing that could have any bearing,' he agreed.

'I'm afraid,' said Glass, 'we'll have to look elsewhere to find out who murdered the happy couple.'

★ ★ ★

When Colin Vickers' father was killed in a car crash, the twelve year old boy and his mother continued to live in the cosy terraced house in Percy Street, Stratford on Avon.

A quarter of a century later they were still there. 'Why would he want to leave?' his mother would tell the neighbours. 'He's got his mother to look after him.' She made no pretence of hoping for a 'nice girl' to come along and marry him.

Colin, of course, would have benefited more from the administrations of a 'bad girl' but, unfortunately, he never found one of these either. Just platonic Glenys.

His mother spoke to him as if he was still twelve, which irritated Colin beyond belief. Many times he had contemplated sticking a carving knife through her heart and, on nights when her snoring kept him awake in the next room, he toyed with the idea of smothering her with a pillow.

But he had never been able to bring himself to do either. So far.

Colin spent Sunday morning in a state of apprehension. The photograph of the girl he had met briefly in the pub had haunted him ever since he'd opened his evening paper.

When it appeared on the morning news on television he almost had apoplexy for, next to it, was an Identikit picture of a man the police wanted to interview.

It looked just like him.

He read the text and learned that a barman had drawn the picture. It must have been the one who came over when the girl had spilt the drink. He'd obviously assumed the two of them were together. How ironic.

Then he remembered he'd picked up the girl's key. If the police found her dead and his prints were on the key . . .

The police would be questioning the bar staff and customers. Any one of his clients could have been in that pub and seen him talking, however briefly, to the girl. His picture on television and in the papers might remind them. The police would easily be able to trace him through his job and when they saw his criminal record, that would be it.

He would have to get away and hide until the police caught the real criminal.

He went up to his room and started packing. He daren't risk taking the company car. He'd drive it to Birmingham this afternoon, leave it in a multi storey somewhere and catch a train to somewhere. He'd worry about the destination later.

None of his customers knew where he lived so he figured he had until Monday morning before the police could get his address from SanDan. By then, he'd be well away.

It didn't occur to him that he'd left his address in the hotel register and he couldn't have known the police were checking out all guests driving blue Mondeos.

Far from having until Monday morning to make his escape, Colin Vickers was just one hour from capture. Even as he packed, Detective Chief Inspector Knox and Detective Sergeant Evans were racing down the M6 towards Stratford.

'Colin, where are you? Your dinner's ready.' His mother's shrill voice rang out from the kitchen.

'Coming, Mum.' He closed the suitcase and ran down the stairs.

'Where've you been? I've been shouting you. Sit down. It's roast beef, your favourite. And I've done you some of those little Yorkshire puddings you like.'

'I'm going to be away for a few days again, Mum,' he said as he picked up his knife and fork. The kitchen was little changed since his father had been alive. Even the pictures on the wall were the same, prints of railway steam engines.

'Not again, son? You've only just got back.'

'Bit of an emergency at work. They've just been on to me.'

'I didn't hear the phone ring,' she said suspiciously.

'No, it was an e-mail.'

Maud Vickers wasn't keen on e-mails. They were too private. She could steam open any hand-written letters that looked personal and she could read faxes that appeared as if by magic out of the telephone, but e-mails defeated her. You couldn't eavesdrop on an e-mail and she couldn't work Colin's computer.

'Well, you need to get a good meal down you before you go. Here, have some more carrots.' She spooned the watery vegetables onto his already crowded plate. 'And have you packed your clean socks?'

Colin Vickers shut his mind off from her non-stop prattle and concentrated on eating his meal. He couldn't wait to get out of the house.

He finished his rice pudding as the Scotland Yard men were turning onto the M42 and by the time they came onto the M40 just seven minutes later, he was putting his case in the car.

'Where did you say you were going this time, son?' His mother was at the door in her apron.

'London.' It was the first place that came into his head.

'Take care then, dear. Don't forget to ring me.'

He kissed her dutifully on the cheek, climbed into the driver's seat and started the engine.

'I won't Mum,' he promised as he eased the car slowly away from the kerb.

He was on the A3400 passing through the picturesque village of Henley in Arden on his way to the M40 northbound as Knox and Evans were coming off the same motorway further south, approaching the Vickers' household from the opposite side of town.

They were driving past the river and the Royal Shakespeare Theatre when they received another call from Superintendent Rimmer. The fingerprints on the door key found in the lock-up had been identified as belonging to Colin Vickers.

'Furthermore, the girl's parents have confirmed the key does belong to Marian. It's the front door key of their house.'

'That's it, then,' said Knox elatedly. 'We've got him.'

'Oddly enough,' went on Rimmer, 'there's no other trace of his prints anywhere in the lock up.'

'He was probably careful,' said Knox. 'But he slipped up with the key.' He thanked the Superintendent and replaced the receiver.

'You think Vickers is Smith then?' asked Sergeant Evans.

'Got to be, hasn't he?'

'He'd hardly be likely to take the girl home to meet his mother though, would he?' Trevor Evans boasted a practical streak.

'Maybe not but he might tell us where he's hidden her.' Once he had made up his mind, Robin Knox was not easily dissuaded. 'Let's hope we're not too late to save her.'

But the time they found Percy Street, they had missed their quarry by thirty minutes.

'He said he was going to London,' a

worried Mrs. Vickers told them. 'He's not in any trouble is he?'

'Did he say where he'd been for the last couple of days?' asked Knox, ignoring her question.

The old lady shook her head. 'The Midlands, I think. He does tell me but I forget. He came home for his tea last night.'

'On his own?'

'Oh yes. He's always on his own is Colin.'

'You haven't got a recent photograph of your son, have you?'

She looked alarmed. 'What do you want that for? What's he done?'

'We think he might be able to help us with some enquires. Nothing to worry about,' replied Knox, blandly. 'A photo would help.'

She gave him a suspicious glare but went obediently to a sideboard in the lounge and extracted a print from a maroon photo album. 'Will this do?'

'Perfect.' It was a head and shoulders portrait, probably taken at a sales conference. 'We'll let you have it back.' He turned to Sergeant Evans.

'Better put a call out for a blue Mondeo heading South on the M40, you've got the registration number. Shouldn't have much trouble picking him up.'

But there he was wrong. At that very moment, Colin Vickers was parking his car in a multi-storey near New Street Station. Within the hour he would be safely on an inter-city train heading out of Birmingham.

18

It was early on Sunday evening at Scotland Yard. The Assistant Commissioner was holding a meeting at which both Detective Chief Inspector Glass and Detective Chief Inspector Knox plus their respective sergeants were present.

The agenda did not make for encouraging reading.

Two actors appearing in a pantomime, starring one of Britain's top comedians, had been savagely murdered, without any obvious motive. Despite extensive police enquiries, no arrests had been made.

Nearly a week after the body of Bath schoolgirl, Judy Whay, was found in a Soho alley, police had still not been able to trace her movements since her disappearance.

Although they knew that the girl was the third known victim of a serial killer, they were no nearer to apprehending the assassin.

Stoke schoolgirl Marian Lynch was still missing but in this case, at least, there was a suspect. Unfortunately, the wanted man had managed to give the police the slip and was now on the run. All forces had been alerted to watch out for his blue Mondeo car but so far, there had been no sightings.

Even the one success of the week, the capture of pornographer Gordon Nightingale, had been marred when the prisoner had hung himself in his cell.

The Assistant Commissioner was not best pleased.

'The newspapers are having a field day,' he raged, holding up a copy of The Sunday Times which bore the headline, what are the police doing? The article asked how many more young girls would be mutilated before the Spa Killer was caught and referred, in passing, to the death of two well-loved actors whose demise also appeared to have police totally baffled.

'I'm looking for results, and soon. We're losing the public's confidence. I shall expect an arrest in the next forty hours or I'll want to know why.'

'I can tell him why, now,' grumbled Glass as they filed out of the room. If we could find the buggers, we'd arrest them. Simple as that. 'What do you say, Robin?'

His son-in-law agreed. 'We must find Vickers soon. Every copper in Britain is watching for his car and his name and photo will be in every paper tomorrow. He operates alone, I can't see anyone hiding him. I give

184

him till noon at latest.'

Detective Chief Inspector Knox was being unduly optimistic. Colin Vickers' car remained unnoticed in the Birmingham multi-storey. Vickers himself, flush with money from the hole in the wall, had caught the Midland Scot to Edinburgh.

He'd never been to the city but he felt he knew it well having read crime novels by Quintin Jardine and Ian Rankin. It seemed to be a very seedy place behind the tourist facade. This suited Vickers well. He liked sleaze.

Hardly had the train left the station before he went into the toilet and shaved off his moustache. When he came out, he moved to a seat in the next carriage so as not to excite suspicion.

By Sunday evening, he was safely ensconced in a small commercial hotel in the city centre where he registered under the name of Bradley. The next morning, he visited a barber and asked for a crew cut. This dramatically changed his appearance as the bald sections of his head were allowed to surface, unencumbered by the Bobby Charlton strands.

He had an anxious moment in the salon when he noticed a photograph of himself on the front page of the morning paper. The police must have been to his home.

His mother would be worried but he wasn't going to ring her. Calls could be traced too easily these days.

Luckily, the elderly barber didn't appear to have looked at the paper. He certainly took little notice of Colin as he snipped away, his only utterance being a guttural comment on the inclement weather.

From Boots the Chemist, Colin purchased a bottle of Clairol colourer which turned his remaining hair a fetching shade of ash blonde.

Dressed in jeans and anorak instead of his usual suit and raincoat, Colin Vickers was unrecognisable from the man whose television picture graced a million Scottish living rooms.

★ ★ ★

It was ten o'clock on Sunday night when Sue Knox served the evening meal to her husband and father.

'I've made pasta,' she said. 'You look like you could do with some energy.'

The strains of the past week's investigations were beginning to show on both policemen. Robin, she thought, looked tired. He was starting to get bags under his eyes and frown lines on his forehead.

186

Her father, too, looked worn out but at least he didn't bottle things up.

'Have a look at this,' Glass said, handing Robin a piece of paper from his wallet.

His son-in-law scrutinised it. 'A python, isn't it? Distinctive markings. What does it mean?'

'I don't know but I'm sure it's significant. I found it on the floor near Gregory Oliver's body.'

'The second dead actor?'

'The same. We found some money too, five hundred pounds in his desk. It wasn't there when we searched the flat after his partner Cadamarteri was killed.'

'Let's have a look at the drawing,' said Sue. Robin passed it over. 'Is it supposed to be in a test tube or what?'

'Search me. I thought it might be a cigar with the picture of a snake on it. Who do we know smokes those?' Glass sighed. 'I don't know, I just felt it might be important.'

'Not necessarily.' It's probably just someone doodling.'

But for once, Detective Chief Inspector Knox was wrong.

★ ★ ★

Marian Lynch spent Sunday in a flat in North London. She didn't know she was in North London. She didn't know it was Sunday. She'd slept throughout the journey from the Potteries and woke at dawn to find herself in a king size bed in a sumptuously furnished room. She was naked.

Julian Swift was watching the room on a closed circuit video monitor in the lounge which also served as an office. It was not Swift's office. He was only here to deliver the girl and assist with the project for which he was being paid an extraordinary amount of money.

The minute Marian awoke, Julian went into her bedroom. 'How are you feeling?' he asked warmly.

'Where am I?'

'At my house,' he lied.

'What am I doing here?'

'You passed out so I brought you back here until you came round. Don't worry, your parents know where you are,' he lied. 'I've said I'll take you home this evening.'

'How did you know how to reach my parents?'

'Their address was in your diary in your satchel.' Julian Swift had always been able to think on his feet.

'What time is it? I want to go home now.' Marian pulled the sheets round her. She was very frightened. She remembered vaguely some terrible photographs being taken of her.

'Not yet, sweetheart. We've got a film to make this afternoon.'

'I'm not doing any more of that.'

Swift's smile was terrifying. 'Oh yes, you are,' he said.

★ ★ ★

The National Westminster Bank confirmed on Monday morning that Gregory Oliver had not drawn any money out of his account in the last five days.

'Where did it come from then?' wondered Sergeant Moon.

'It wasn't his birthday,' said Detective Chief Inspector Glass. 'And he hadn't won the Lottery. It's got to be blackmail hasn't it?'

'But who? What did two harmless old men know that was so dangerous it got them both killed?'

'If we knew that, Moon, we'd know the name of the murderer.'

'So it's back to the cast is it?'

'Nothing else to go on. There's a rehearsal this afternoon to integrate the two new actors so we'll get down there. At this rate, we'll be offered a part in the show.'

However, an afternoon of intensive

questioning brought them nothing new. Most of the cast had been lying late in bed after the Saturday show and not all of them were able to provide a witness to the event.

'This time I do have an alibi,' Harry Hooper informed him. They were in his star dressing room and Hooper was in his Alice the Cook costume again, this time a silver lame dress of Dame Edna Everage style. 'A young lady dancer from my television show was with me from midnight until late afternoon.'

'I'm very pleased for you, sir,' said Glass who would probably have preferred the girl's mother. 'And I take it that you didn't leave her side in all that time?'

'We were glued together,' beamed the comedian, 'metaphorically speaking of course.'

Glass ignored the man's swagger. 'I'd like you to recall every bit of conversation you had with both the deceased men during the course of this production.'

Hooper took a sip of gin and tonic from a glass on the dressing table. 'Very little, actually. We exchanged pleasantries. Max gave me a tip for the King George. Suny Bay, as a matter of fact. You ought to back it, Inspector. Max was pretty good with his tips. It could win.'

This time Glass ignored his demotion.

'What about Mr. Oliver?'

'No, he was never into the gee-gees.'

'I mean, what about your conversations with him?'

'Confined to 'cold for the time of year, dearie.' ' Harry giggled. 'Look, they were a couple of fairies, nice enough in their way but not my sort of people. What was it we said, Inspector? Ring a ring of roses, hah, hah.' He gave a throaty laugh. 'No, we just happened to be in the same show, that's all.'

'Something we didn't think of, sir,' said Sergeant Moon as they left the comedian. 'Gambling. He could have won that £500 on the horses.'

Glass had to admit that was a possibility. 'We'll have to check with all the bookies in the area but Hooper did say it was Max not Gregory that was the racing man.'

'What about local meetings? He could have put the bets on at the course.'

'I can't see him going to a race meeting so soon after Max Cadamarteri's death. He was too upset.'

'Maybe it was Cadamarteri who won the money.'

'Then why didn't we find it before?'

Sergeant Moon was silent. There was no answer to that.

The policemen moved on. Jim Smith, the

Wicked Baron, once again proffered his wife to substantiate his claim to have been in the house all day.

'I can't pretend I'm mourning,' he said, defiantly. 'It's two less of the slime, isn't it? But I wouldn't have wished them harm on a personal level.'

Sergeant Moon, who had a more liberal philosophy than his Inspector, looked like he was having difficulty restraining himself from making a comment so Glass hurried them along to Jack's dressing room.

'Jack', alias Marsha Flint, had been boating with friends on The Serpentine. They had then gone for a meal in the West End followed by a film in Leicester Square. Her friends would confirm this.

The rest of the cast was at home sleeping, cooking or watching television. Most of them on their own.

Sergeant Moon was quite depressed about it all. 'So any one of a dozen of them had the opportunity?'

'All of them if the witnesses were lying.'

'And no sign of blackmail.'

'None that we can see.'

'Something will turn up,' predicted Glass. 'It always does.'

And it did but not from the direction Glass anticipated.

19

Gordon Nightingale's suicide had brought the enquiry into Himmler Films to a full stop. At least for the moment. The people involved in the film with Linzi Pennington were charged with as many offences relating to indecency, assault on police officers and abduction of a minor that Detective Chief Inspector Glass thought the Crown Prosecution Service would accept, and subsequently released on bail.

One of the men, the Schwarzeneggar look-alike, requested an audience with the detective. He wanted to do a deal.

'I don't do deals,' Glass informed him when they met at Scotland Yard on Monday evening, 'unless I benefit substantially from them.'

'You're looking for the person who killed the Bath schoolgirl?'

Suddenly Glass was all attention. 'Not personally but I can pass any messages on.'

'Look, I want to be an actor. I did that stuff for cash but I really want to get into proper films and the theatre.'

'Do you indeed? Well, I know somebody who's looking for two people to play a pantomime cow. With a dick as big as yours, you could probably manage both halves.' He thrust his face inches from the other's nose. 'Don't come that bullshit with me. You don't beat up under-age schoolgirls and pretend it's acting.'

'At least I don't kill them.'

'What?'

'That girl they found in Soho.'

'Judy Whay? How does she come into this?'

'She did the films like I did.'

'You knew her?'

'No, but I saw her photo in the paper and I recognised her.

'When was this?'

'A few weeks ago. In Bristol, it was. I went down for a day's filming and she was on the set.'

'I take it by 'filming' you mean something similar to the set up with Linzi Pennington?'

'Was that her name?'

'Yes it was.' The man's insouciance infuriated Glass. 'What you mean is a bondage film? S. & M.'

'Erotic art, if you don't mind. That's what they'd call it at Cannes. They award Oscars now for porn, didn't you know?'

Glass had always thought the world was going crazy. Now he knew he was right.

'They'll be giving medals for shitting next. Wouldn't make it any more acceptable. Now tell me who made this film.'

'The Bristol area manager, of course.' He saw the policeman's blank expression and laughed. 'I see you know nothing about the system.'

'What system's that?'

'Why, Himmler Films of course. Didn't Mr. Nightingale explain it all to you?' Glass said nothing but thought that if Gordon Nightingale hadn't already hanged himself, he might have done it for him.

'Oh yes,' continued the actor who called himself 'Big Ben', 'Gordon was the West Region area manager in London. He found the girls, booked the studios, brought in the scripts and sent off the finished masterpiece back to Head Office.'

'Which is where?'

'Sorry, officer. Got me there. I never had anything to do with that side of it myself. Like I told you, I'm just the stud in all this.'

'And was Judy a willing participant?'

'Yes. It was early days, of course. She'd only been doing it for a short while, a few weeks or so. And, of course, she was madly in love with the Bristol bloke. That's how they recruit new girls.'

195

'But when things get heavy and the girls want to stop?'

'They can't.' The bald statement said it all.

'So if you're nothing more than a stud, as you quaintly put it, how can you offer me anything in a deal?'

'I know the name of the Bristol Area Manager. He was there at the shoot.'

'How many area managers are there?'

'They're all over the country. The Bristol fellow covers Bath and Bristol.'

'And you're telling me he had something to do with her murder?'

'Let's say I've heard rumours that some of the actresses don't always make it to the last reel.'

Glass was horrified, both by the information and by the casual way it was mentioned. 'Have you been a witness to any such occasion?'

'Snuff films, you mean. Not me. I just go for plain and simple screwing.'

'With a whip?'

'Well, maybe a bit of mild bondage.' Glass remembered Linzi's bruises and fought back a desire to book the man a permanent bed in Stoke Mandeville Hospital.

'So. Do we have a deal then?' asked 'Big Ben', whose real name was Gavin Davis.

'You drop the charges, I give you the info. on the Bristol connection.' He made it sound like something out of a spy novel.

'If we pick him up from the information you give us, I'll do my best to have the charges put on file. If we don't get him, I'll have you for accessory to murder.'

'You can't do that.'

'Try me.' 'Ben' saw the expression on the other's face and knew he meant it. He pondered for a minute. He wasn't over-bright. As his teachers had often pointed out to him prior to his expulsion from his comprehensive schools, most of his brains were in his trousers.

'OK, done. You better stick to it though.'

'Or . . . ?' Glass moved threateningly forward. The man born Gavin Davis backed down.

'The bloke you want is Benny Jackson. I believe he used to be a jockey before he took up with Himmlers.' It was a name he'd overheard once in conversation. Davis thought you never knew when things like that would come in useful.

'Where will I find him?'

'I don't know his home address but the studio he used is in Bristol, near St. Paul's. I think he may have an office there.' He gave the policeman the address. 'Tell your boys to be careful. Jackson can be a nasty piece of work. The sort who enjoys the films, if you know what I mean.'

'And you don't?'

'Big Ben' shrugged. 'Pays for the designer trainers, don't it?'

'This better be kosher,' warned the detective. 'Or you could be playing the lead in *Mary Poppins*.'

The actor smiled. 'I've always fancied Dick Van Dyke. Women are strictly for work, Chief Inspector,' and to Glass's disgust, he blew him a kiss as he walked away.

Detective Chief Inspector Glass sought out Sergeant Moon. 'I want you in at seven prompt tomorrow morning. We're going a drive to Bristol.'

'Is this to do with the theatre, sir?'

'It's to do with acting, Moon. Acting of a sort, that is.' He recounted his interview with Gavin Davis. 'It's our first lead.'

'Why didn't Nightingale tell us all this?'

'Perhaps he really didn't know. The people at the top of this organisation seem to keep their staff at arm's length. Nightingale might not have known he was one of many of these so-called Area Managers. What the minions don't know they can't tell. But I'll find out who's running Himmler Films if it kills me.'

★ ★ ★

Marian Lynch spent the whole of Monday on set. The bedroom in which she was imprisoned served as a backdrop for Himmler Film's latest production.

Directing an epic called *Teachers' Treats* was Julian Swift, the Potteries' Area Manager for Himmler Films.

A camera crew had moved in along with the only prop, a blackboard on an easel. Most of the action was to take place on the king-size bed.

Marion had eaten a light breakfast which consisted of some toast and marmalade and a cup of tea containing another 'roofie'. She was therefore in a compliant mood when joined by her fellow actors.

The teacher was played by a stocky man in his fifties who had a scar down the side of his stubbled right cheek and a gold tooth. Even dressed in a gown and mortarboard he looked more like a pirate.

Marian had been naked since she arrived at the flat but now Julian gave her back her school clothes to put on.

She didn't notice the front door key was missing from her blouse pocket.

Even under the effects of the drug, the young girl became agitated when two other 'teachers' joined in the action and took turns in possessing her. All of them were older than her father. None of them used a condom.

But all of them used the cane!

Julian Swift called a wrap at four o'clock, well pleased with the day's work. So pleased that when he sent off the videos to Himmler's head office he put in a little note recommending Marian for the Special Treatment.

As he sealed the Jiffy bag, he wondered why Himmler had changed their name to Mother Teresa Films and had a new box office number but it wasn't really his concern.

All he did was find the girls, make the films and collect the cash.

If Marian was selected, Julian Swift would receive a big bonus.

If Marian were selected, she would be following in the footsteps of Emma Turner, Maxine Berry and Judy Whay. Footsteps that led to the grave.

Unless she was rescued in time.

20

David Osbourne was born and brought up in the genteel Yorkshire spa town of Harrogate, the only child of a professional couple who lived in a large stone detached house on the edge of The Stray. David attended the local grammar school where he achieved excellent 'A' levels in economics, classics and mathematics and subsequently gained a place at Oxford University.

When his careers master asked him what he wanted to do with his life, he replied truthfully that he had no idea. He would consider anything at all, he said, but with one proviso. It had to make him a multi-millionaire before he was thirty.

He studied Sunday Times list of the country's five hundred richest men and came to a few conclusions.

First of all, you had to work for yourself. The business world was full of Harvard-trained middle managers on high salaries but likely to be redundant at forty.

Secondly, education counted for nothing. The people who made the real money were more likely to start by selling ice cream from a milk bar at thirteen like Charles Forte.

Thirdly, any professional career might make you rich but it was a marathon not a sprint. He wanted the big money now.

David Osbourne eschewed the opportunity to go to Oxford.

Assuming he wasn't going to be a pop star or international sportsman, his money would have to be made through business, either inside or outside the law.

After studying all the options, he came to the conclusion that the best opportunities lay in areas, which served the three basic human needs, namely food, shelter and sex.

He could have added drugs, which would soon become a fourth basic need if the escalation in use amongst young people continued, but, strangely, he had a moral objection to their use.

Food and property, he felt, were tied up by the conglomerates and the chances of starting from scratch and making a quick fortune grew smaller every year.

Which left sex.

Osbourne had seen how people like Paul Raymond and David Sullivan had built up huge empires on the back of the public's obsession with sex. Boundaries of taste and decency were being pushed back ever further as, one by one, age-old taboos were abolished.

He had observed that once a forbidden subject became openly talked about, often beginning with moral outrage, that subject soon became acceptable. The public disgust would soon be replaced by curiosity and then the floodgates would open and something once never mentioned was suddenly accepted as commonplace. Like, for example, oral sex.

David could foresee a time when all film stars would be required to have sex openly on screen as people looked for more outrageous thrills to satisfy their increasing sexual appetites, fuelled by constant bombardment by advertisers and the media.

Which meant, the porn industry would have to go further.

He checked out the 'adult' magazines on the newsagents' top shelves and noticed there seemed to be a growing demand for 'amateur' publications such as 'Readers' Wives' featuring imperfect models rather than the airbrushed professionals that previously adorned the glamour pages.

He was amazed that so many people were prepared to submit quite revealing snapshots of their often indescribably ugly spouses. He noticed, too, that the magazines often mentioned that the models would be surprised, even distressed, to know their unclothed features were displayed in a popular magazine on sale throughout the land. This seemed to add to the appeal, as if the readers were seeing something they weren't supposed to.

David Osbourne realised that this army of peeping toms, pathetic though he might regard them, offered considerable commercial potential to someone with the right product to sell.

He invested in a video camera and took films of a succession of willing young ladies who were seduced by his bright blue eyes, easy charm and Mercedes convertible. Those who weren't so willing were persuaded either by protestations of undying love or a large quantity of alcoholic beverages. Or by a combination of both.

Soon he had built up a sizeable collection of videos that he sold without trouble around the North Yorkshire area. But this was not enough for Osbourne who wanted to operate on a national scale.

His big problem was distribution. He had no means of getting the stuff into the shops in the rest of the country. Then, somebody told him about an outfit called Himmler Films based in London who ran a big pornography operation.

David spoke to their main man on the phone and they agreed a deal. Business soon exceeded all expectations and the man, whom David knew only as Carlos, demanded more product.

David started advertising in various magazines for amateur videos. He offered top money, the more bizarre or explicit the film, the higher the price. He soon found that the biggest demand was for so-called bondage films, from mild flagellation to full S & M horrors.

His next step was to appoint agents, or Area Managers, as he called them, to run their own territories and procure more actors.

He was soon providing Himmler Films with a significant proportion of their catalogue as production rapidly grew.

He was just twenty-two when he met a computer programmer called Sylvia Harrison. She was four years older than he and one of an increasing number of women who were highly computer literate. She was pretty good at sex too.

She soon taught David Osbourne everything she knew about both subjects. For a while, he considered branching out into computer hacking. The idea of transferring large sums of money from a bank into his own account, without the bank even knowing about it, appealed to him greatly. However, the prospect of a long jail sentence if he was caught acted as an efficient deterrent.

But he became very excited about the exploitation of sex through computers, particularly interactive sex on the Internet.

Instead of going out to buy the films, people could watch them on-line merely by giving their credit card number. And this was live action. Customers could actually dictate what they wanted to happen in the film.

Thousands of hookers the world over realised they could provide the services their clients required from a safe distance, without ever having to meet such unpleasant people in the flesh.

Likewise, punters were able to have their needs satisfied without the fear of being caught in brothel raids, mugged by pimps or inflicted with unpleasant social diseases, even if they had to do all the work themselves.

It was an idea that was perfect for its time.

David Osbourne was twenty-three and well on the way to making his first million.

He didn't live to see twenty-four.

His big mistake was to exclude Carlos from the credit card and Internet part of the business. Carlos felt slighted when the omission was brought to his attention and he was not a man who took kindly to being rebuffed.

He didn't carry out the assassination himself. Instead, he arranged a rendezvous with David on the top floor of a central London multi-storey car park and sent along the hired killer.

David didn't see the huge four wheel drive car bearing down on him across the deserted car park until it was too late. He threw himself to one side but the driver was able to turn the wheel in time and crush him beneath it.

The coroner's verdict was a satisfactory one — accidental death. David Osbourne had been killed under the wheels of a Jeep Cherokee whose driver did not stop and was never traced.

The president of Himmler Films took over the Internet operation and built on it. Soon scenes of incredible degradation were being enacted live on-screen in accordance with the depraved wishes of hundreds of paying customers and relayed via cyberspace to every corner of the earth.

Whether or not the actresses, and actors, were willing.

Roland Pawson ran a video rental business with branches in Bath, Bristol and Cheltenham. He was a diminutive man, barely five foot four, with thinning brown hair and traces of a Welsh accent.

Like most small shopkeepers, he didn't find it easy to make a living in competition with the big chains but he had the advantage that some of the videos he offered to selected customers were of a kind not readily available at Blockbusters or the local public library.

These videos he purchased from a company called Himmler Films who sent him a brochure of new releases each month with graphic descriptions of the contents and suitably erotic colour pictures to accompany them.

There were no addresses or telephone numbers listed anywhere on the literature. Pawson gave his orders to the Himmler rep, Barry Jackson, who called at regular intervals with new catalogues and collected money for advance orders.

Roland noticed that one of the films in the latest catalogue he'd received the previous evening was called *Playground Pets*. He could think of at least a couple of his regulars who would enjoy that one. One of them was his old gym master.

In the section marked 'Forthcoming Features' he observed a film called *Classroom Capers*. The picture beside it was of a pretty girl in a blue striped blazer and light blue blouse with her hair in bunches tied with blue ribbon. She looked about fourteen. The blouse was undone to the waist and she wore no bra but her school tie was strategically placed to cover her nipples.

In her mouth was the erect penis of a gentleman of West Indian persuasion.

Pawson stopped to examine the photo more closely. He was sure he'd seen that same girl here in his shop in Bath.

Curious, he turned to his computer, brought up on screen his database of members and reorganised them into place order. He had an idea the girl was called Judy or Julie. He scrolled through the Bath list until he came to the name he was looking for.

He was right but he checked with last week's copy of the Bath Chronicle to make sure and there was her photograph on the front page.

Judy Whay. The missing schoolgirl who'd been found dead in London.

He wondered if the police knew. He had a contact in the Bristol police who made sure his premises were never raided in return for any scraps of useful information that came his way. He was even known to pay reasonable sums of money if the information was of enough value to him.

Quentin thought this might be worth fifty pounds to him at least. He telephoned the police station and spoke to his uniformed friend.

An hour later, the policeman came into the Bath premises of Pawson Video Libraries and followed the proprietor into the back room where he was shown the December Himmler catalogue. He was careful not to mention Barry Jackson. He wanted to reach retirement with his limbs intact. Instead, he told his friend Sergeant Prole that the catalogue had arrived in the post.

But there was no reward for Roland Pawson. Instead, the policeman confiscated the catalogue and returned to the station where he immediately telephoned Scotland Yard to speak to the officer in charge of the case of The Spa Killer.

He was put though to Detective Chief Inspector Robin Knox.

It was eleven o'clock on Tuesday morning. 'We'll be with you by lunchtime,' replied Knox.

21

Detective Chief Inspector Glass and Detective Sergeant Moon made the early morning trip to Bristol in Glass's Morris Traveller. 'I thought I'd call in at the Morris Minor Centre and get it valued while we're there.'

'Not thinking of selling it, are you?' asked Moon, surprisingly. 'You've always liked these old . . . ' he was going to say bangers but quickly changed his mind, ' . . . these classic cars.'

'I don't like classic cars,' barked Glass. 'I like old bangers like this one and my old Mini Countryman. Only I've seen a Standard Eight I liked the look of.'

Moon groaned. They were already flat out at 55 m.p.h. The journey to Bristol in a Standard Eight would be a two-day trip. He wouldn't be surprised if the inspector's next purchase was a horse.

They stopped on the M4 services near Theale for a late breakfast, Glass making the most of his expense account by filling his corpulent stomach with a cholesterol-packed accumulation of fried foodstuffs. Sergeant Moon favoured a raisin croissant and a weak tea.

Even allowing for the limitations of the vehicle and the motorway stop, they did the 117-mile trip in three hours, reaching Bristol shortly after ten thirty. It didn't take long for them to find the address given to them by Gavin 'Big Ben' Davis.

Portland Studios was on the first floor above a dingy parade of shops, its entrance lying between run-down newsagents and a greengrocer.

'I wouldn't care to eat any of those,' declared Glass, pointing to bunches of black bananas on a table marked 'reduced' by the door.

The sign on the door informed them that Portland Studios were for hire at favourable terms and also supplied photographers for portraits, weddings and important social gatherings.

'They probably mean gang bangs,' said Glass as they climbed the steep, narrow stairs. A glass door awaited them at the top behind which sat a lady at a reception desk. She was well past her prime although she had made a valiant, albeit unsuccessful, attempt with vivid make-up to recapture her fading looks and the leather mini skirt that revealed her bulging cellulite thighs suggested she wouldn't give in without a fight.

Glass fancied her immediately.

'Can I help you?'

'We're looking for Mr. Jackson.'

'Is that Benny or Perry?'

'Benny, please.'

'Who shall I say wants him?'

'Detective Chief Inspector Glass from Scotland Yard.' He flashed his ID in front of her face. 'Brothers are they?'

'Father and son.' She spoke into the phone. 'Benny. Two policemen to see you. Should I send them through?'

There was a pause. Benny was obviously considering his best plan of action. Or getting rid of questionable merchandise. Glass took the opportunity to study the receptionist and wondered why women who kept their hair below shoulder length to retain the illusion of youth, then allowed it to go naturally grey. Hadn't she heard of peroxide?'

'He'll see you, if you'd like to go through. Last door on the right.'

It was obvious why Benny Jackson was an ex-jockey. Even a Shire horse might have objected to being saddled with such a bulk on its back. He had long blond hair and matching beard through which a set of large horse-like teeth protruded.

Moon wondered if it was true that people grew to look like their animals.

'Good morning Mr. Jackson.' Glass flashed

his ID card again, introduced himself and his companion, and held out his hand warmly. He was always at his most dangerous when affable. 'Thank you for agreeing to see us without an appointment.'

'What is it you want?' Jackson did not seem to share his visitor's desire for cordiality.

Glass produced a picture from his pocket. 'Have you seen this young lady at all, sir?'

Jackson gave a cursory glance at the features of Judy Whay. 'No. Should I have done?'

'Her picture's been published all over the national newspapers and television for the past week.'

'I've seen it. But I haven't seen her. The girl, that is.' His voice was rough and uneducated.

'That's odd.' Glass was still smiling. 'Only I have a man in custody back at Scotland Yard who has made a statement to the effect that he was present when you made a pornographic film of Judy Whay in this very studio only last month.'

Jackson's cheeks turned deep red, the veins next to his temples began to throb and his clenched knuckles were white. For a moment, Moon thought he was going to attack them but he restrained himself.

'It's all fucking lies. I've never seen her.'

'Then you'll have no objection if we search your studio?' Glass dug again in his pocket and pulled out a piece of paper. 'I expect you'll want to examine the search warrant, sir. Maybe you'll want your solicitor present too. This is, after all, a murder enquiry.'

Sergeant Moon did not recall the Inspector applying for a search warrant. The paper he was waving about looked suspiciously like a receipt for his dry-cleaning. He hoped this was not going to be one of Glass's famous bluffs. One day he could foresee terrible consequences to his superior's modus operandi.

But not this time.

'Search all you fucking like, you'll find nothing. I've never seen the bint. Here, take my keys.' He threw a bunch of keys at the two policemen. 'I'll show you where to start.' As he spoke, he pushed past them and strode out of the room, slamming the door after him and dextrously turning a key in the lock from the opposite side.

Glass had stooped to pick up the bunch of keys that had fallen on the floor, Moon tried to run past him just as Glass was rising and the two officers fell to the floor in a tangled heap.

Sergeant Moon, being younger and fitter, was the first to scramble to his feet. He rushed to the window, which overlooked a back yard, just in time to see Barry Jackson getting into his car and driving away.

The car was a blue Mondeo.

★ ★ ★

Robin Knox had no idea his father-in-law was in Bristol when he and Sergeant Evans pulled up outside the city centre police station shortly after one o'clock.'

'We've got an appointment with Sergeant Prole,' Robin told the desk sergeant, 'I'm Detective Chief Inspector Knox from Scotland Yard.'

'Haydn Prole? Oh yes, I believe he's expecting you. Hang on, I'll ring him.'

Sergeant Prole came to greet them a minute later. He was six foot three, darkhaired and spoke with a distinct West Country accent.

'Have you eaten?' he asked them, 'only there's a little pub round the corner. We could have a bite to eat whilst I tell you about Mr. Pawson.'

'Sounds good to me,' said Robin.

Once the food had been ordered and the drinks served, Prole put them in the picture with regard to Pawson's video shop operation then showed them the copy of the Himmler

216

Film Catalogue he had taken from Roland Pawson.

'That's her isn't it?' he said, pointing to the schoolgirl star of *Classroom Capers*. 'Judy Whay.'

'That's her all right.' Knox turned over the pages of the catalogue. Suddenly, Sergeant Evans, who was sitting on the other side of him, grabbed the book from him.

'That's Linzi,' he exclaimed, snatching the book from the Chief Inspector's grasp. 'My goddaughter.' The page was open at *Playground Pets*. 'I don't believe it,' he groaned. 'What if her parents see this? Where does it come from?'

'I've been through it from cover to cover,' said Sergeant Prole. 'There's no address anywhere.'

'If this came from a video shop,' pointed out Knox, 'the owner will know where to order the films from.'

'I'll take you to see him after we've had our meal,' offered Prole. 'He's called Roland Pawson. He's got a shop here in Bristol and one in Cheltenham as well.' He lowered his voice. 'As a matter of fact, he's one of my informers. He comes up with some good information from time to time.'

'And in return, you turn a blind eye to his blue film transactions?'

'Exactly. Mind you, it's only small time stuff. As soon as I saw the Whay girl's photo in there, I was on to you. Porn's one thing, murder another matter entirely.'

Sergeant Evans didn't look as if he totally agreed with this. His strict Methodist upbringing did not allow for public licentiousness on any scale.

'Ah, here's the food,' said Knox, gratefully. Trevor Evans looked like he couldn't wait to get his hands on Roland Pawson and anyone else connected with his goddaughter's screen activities. 'I think the salmon's mine. Let's get this eaten, then we can get to Pawson's shop. He was anxious to follow-up the only lead that he had in the Judy Whay case.

The short drive from Bristol to Bath took them twenty minutes. Roland Pawson's shop was near Twerton, not far from Bristol Rovers football ground.

They parked on the road outside and the three of them marched up to the front door.

'That's strange, it's locked,' said Sergeant Prole.

Sergeant Evans consulted the sign on the door. 'According to this, they open from nine thirty in the morning to eleven at night. You said he has three branches. Could he be in one of the others?'

'He could be but he's usually in Bath on a Tuesday and he was here this morning when he gave me that catalogue. Besides, if he weren't here, one of his staff would be running the shop. It wouldn't be shut.'

'The sign says 'Open',' observed Knox. 'Something's wrong. Is there any other way in?'

'There'll be a back entrance. He lives above the shop.'

'What are we waiting for? Let's go.' They sprinted to the end of the street and round into an alley that ran behind the row of shops. In their haste, none of the policeman noticed a blue Mondeo parked beside the pavement between a Fiesta and a Renault Megane.

'This'll be the one,' said Haydn Prole, stopping outside a back yard gate. 'It's the same maroon coloured paint.' He took hold of the latch. 'It's locked. Give me a hand up.' Evans cupped his hands and the Bristol man vaulted from them over the gate and unlocked it to let them into the back yard.

There was no sign of life. 'Back door's locked,' said Prole unnecessarily. 'Windows all shut. Should we get a search warrant.'

'No need to. We've every reason to believe a crime has been committed here.' None of them needed to be told what sort of crime that was.

'Let me.' Sergeant Evans couldn't wait to get his hands on anyone remotely connected with Himmler Films. The back door yielded to his burly boots at the third attempt.

'You're becoming an expert in house-breaking,' commented Knox, remembering the sergeant's successful admittance to the Stoke Business Park.

'It never seems to prove very productive though,' replied Evans, as they ran through the living quarters to the shop at the front. The place was deserted.

'Let's try upstairs.'

By this time, they were all expecting to find the remains of Roland Pawson but in this they were disappointed. The house was completely empty.

'The Marie Celeste part two,' said Knox.

'He could always be at one of the other branches.'

They went back into the shop. 'The phone numbers are on that list on the wall,' said Evans.

Sergeant Prole picked up the telephone, dialled the Cheltenham branch of Pawson Video Libraries and asked to speak to Roland Pawson.

'I'm sorry, he isn't here,' said a girl's voice.

'You should find him at our Bath shop. Do you want the number?'

'Thanks, I've already got it.' Prole replaced the receiver and dialled the Bristol branch. He got a similar reply.

'They seem to be operating normally,' he said. 'But our Mr. Pawson has vanished into thin air.'

Detective Chief Inspector Knox grimaced. Every time they had a lead, something went wrong. Colin Vickers had disappeared without trace. Now Pawson.

He realised now, for the first time, that the Spa Killer case was tied up with his father-in-law's investigation. Himmler Films was the link between the two. But Glass's witness had disappeared too and in Gordon Nightingale's case, he wouldn't be coming back.

The big question was, of course, was Marian Lynch another Himmler victim? If she was, then Colin Vickers was not the lonely misfit that Otis Ellis predicted but part of a sophisticated criminal organisation.

Either way, Marian was still missing and in obvious danger.

'Put out an alert,' Robin told Sergeant Prole. 'I don't know how much Pawson knows but he's either running scared or someone's trying to shut him up. If they haven't already,' he added grimly. 'We'll get

221

back to London, but keep me informed.'

Sergeant Prole drove them back to police headquarters and the two Scotland Yard men picked up their car for the return trip down the M4.

'We're one step behind all along the way in this investigation,' said Knox to Sergeant Evans. 'Every time we get a lead, we're too late.

'Walter Glass has been on the Himmler case,' said Trevor Evans. 'I wonder how far he's got with it?'

He was not to know that Glass, too, was in Bristol armed with the same picture of Judy Whay and faring just as badly as they were.

22

Detective Chief Inspector Glass and Sergeant Moon might well have echoed Robin Knox's sentiments about being too late.

It was a full two minutes before Benny Jackson's ageing secretary opened the door to release them from his office, by which time the Mondeo had well disappeared from sight.

'Where's he gone?' Glass shouted at her.

'Do you mean Mr. Jackson?' she enquired innocently.

'Who the hell else is there in here?' bellowed Glass.

'Just myself. Is there anything I can help you with Chief Inspector?'

'We have reason to believe there is pornographic material on these premises. Sergeant Moon and myself intend to conduct a search forthwith.'

The lady stood her ground. 'I don't think so,' she said.

'What?' Glass could hardly believe she was defying him.

'I mean, I don't think there's anything here of the nature you describe.' She gave him a sweet smile. 'But you're willing to look.

Would you care for a cup of tea?'

'Just a little milk with no sugar,' replied Glass quickly. 'The colour of an African woman. And Sergeant Moon would like his milky. What did you say your name was, by the way?'

'I didn't. But it's Lillian Jackson. I'm Benny's mother.'

'What! You never told us that.'

'You never asked me, Chief Inspector. My husband started this business and now my son runs it and I answer the phone. A real family business you might say. May I ask what evidence you have to warrant this visit?'

Glass ignored the question and, instead, pulled out of his wallet the photograph of Judy Whay. 'Have you ever seen this girl on these premises?'

She studied almost too obviously. 'Never. Isn't that the poor girl from Bath who was found murdered in London?'

'That's the one.'

'I read about it in the papers. It was horrible. But she's never been here, I can assure you. Whoever told you she has has misinformed you.'

Glass didn't believe Gavin Davis had lied to him but he was convinced of Mrs. Jackson's mendacity. He allowed her to make the tea whilst he and Sergeant Moon went through the desks, shelves and cupboards of the offices and studio.

'We'll find nothing,' he whispered to Moon. 'She wouldn't have let us search the place if there'd been anything they didn't want us to find. We might as well go through the motions though. When we've had the tea, we'll go.'

They went through the motions and the detective was right. They found nothing incriminating. 'Tell your son that we'd like to interview him at his earliest convenience,' smiled Glass sweetly, as he returned his empty mug. 'He had to leave before we had chance for a little chat.'

'That was a waste of time,' said Moon as they left the building.

'Nice cup of tea, though,' commented Glass, 'and cheaper than McDonalds. Did you get the car number?'

Moon handed across a slip of paper.

'Good lad. We'll ring Bristol police and ask them to put out an alert.'

Their next stop was the Morris Minor Centre where Glass was given a valuation for his vehicle that made him even more depressed.

'It's the rust, you see,' the mechanic there told him. 'And the wood's rotted in several places caused by water getting behind the joints.' The mechanic was not impressed by the engine either. 'A hundred thousand's nothing for these but two hundred's pushing it. Mechanically, I'd say it was decidedly dodgy. And being hand-painted doesn't help its chances. Whatever made you do it purple?'

'It was that colour when I bought it,' said Glass, glumly.

'How much did you give for it, sir, if you don't mind me asking?'

'I do,' barked Glass, insulted, and they took their leave.

The mechanic's gloomy prognosis seemed justified, however, very soon afterwards when the Morris Traveller developed a choking noise in the engine and started to lose power shortly after they joined the motorway. They had progressed hardly a mile along the M4 when the car finally spluttered to a stop. Glass managed to glide it on to the hard shoulder.

'Are you in the AA?' asked Moon, thinking the horse and cart may have been a better bet.

'No,' said Glass. 'It's never broken down before.'

However, he needn't have worried. Salvation was at hand. By an amazing coincidence, at that very moment, a police car came speeding along the carriageway and pulled up alongside.

'Want a push, sir,' said Detective Chief Inspector Robin Knox.

★ ★ ★

'Let's see exactly what we've got so far.' They were halfway to London and had fully acquainted each other with their progress, or lack of it, on their respective trips to the West Country.

Robin had radioed Sergeant Prole at Bristol police station and arranged for a local garage to pick up his father-in-law's Morris Traveller. He'd also advised him about Benny Jackson and the call-out on the Mondeo.

But Sergeant Prole had already had news of the Mondeo. 'It was found less than five minutes ago, parked outside Pawson's shop.'

'But we've just been there ourselves.'

'Exactly. The traffic lads said the engine was cold though, so it must have been there then. We didn't notice it but, then, we weren't looking for it. We'd other things on our minds.'

'So the inference is that Benny Jackson's

taken Pawson away, with or without his consent. Does Jackson know Pawson's a grass?'

'Quite possibly,' replied Haydn Prole.

'In that case,' said Knox. 'I don't give much for his chances. These are ruthless people. Check what car Pawson drives, they might have gone off in that, and let us know if you find them.' He shut off the phone.

'We've managed a hat-trick of cock-ups,' announced Glass. 'That's where we're up to. I can see the Assistant Commissioner loving us when we get back.'

'We've got to look at it positively. What do we know so far?'

'Nightingale, Jackson and Vickers are all agents for this Himmler Films outfit. One's dead and the other two are missing and now the bloody salesman's been abducted. That's as positive as you'll get.'

Glass wished he hadn't given up smoking. At times like this he missed his Craven A which used to irritate his throat and so take his mind off his problems.

'We know that Judy Whay was involved with them so it follows that the Buxton and Llandudno killings are down to the Himmler people too.'

'And Marian Lynch,' broke in Sergeant Evans.

'Ah, we don't know that for sure,' said Knox, defensively. 'It is possible that Marian Lynch is a separate case altogether. This Colin Vickers sounds just like the sort of psychopathic loner that Otis Ellis talked about.'

'Possible,' conceded Glass, 'but remote, I'd say. No, Vickers will be in with them. What have you got from the girl's parents and school friends?'

'Zilch.'

'I think the injuries have a meaning,' said Sergeant Moon, speaking up for the first time. 'I think they're part of the film script.'

Trevor Evans' face tightened at this. Had 'Playground Pets' not been shown at the Police Christmas Party, Linzi Pennington could well have become one of the Spa Killer's victims. 'I hope you're wrong,' he said. 'Otherwise, God help that poor kid.'

23

Benny Jackson drove away from his studio a worried man, yet the fact that he'd imprisoned two Scotland Yard detectives and was on the run from the police was the least of his problems.

Benny had worked for Himmler Films for several months but not until the murder of Judy Whay did he realise just what he'd got himself into.

Benny's main problem was that he'd been born with the twin handicaps of a nasty disposition and the intelligence of a mentally retarded goat, a fatal combination.

His father had built up a prosperous little business with his photographic studio and Perry Jackson had hoped his son would follow in his footsteps but Benny had had other ideas. For some unaccountable reason, he wanted to be a National Hunt jockey.

He was taken on as a stable lad by a trainer in Somerset but his surly manner did not endear him to the others on the yard. The horses, too, were not keen on the new arrival. Apart from being a burden for them to carry, he used his whip on them at every opportunity, on and off the racecourse. On the few occasions he was given a ride, Benny Jackson saw little of the Winner's Enclosure.

He stuck it for two years but, in the end, it was the weight problem that finally put paid to Benny's riding career and he was left at twenty-one with no educational qualifications and no job.

Inevitably, he ended up in the family business and it was in one of his father's video magazines that he saw the same advertisement that had caught Gordon Nightingale's eye.

He wrote for details to Himmler Films at the box office number given and he soon found there was more money to be made in pornography than wedding albums.

He enticed a succession of young girls into his studio, usually at night when his father had gone home. If he hadn't got the looks and charm to seduce them, he certainly had the money.

Once his credentials with Himmler had been established, the company started to send him storylines to enact, involving a larger cast. He had enough dubious friends and willing girls to oblige them.

It didn't worry him when the films he was asked to make became more violent or bizarre. He just paid the girls more money or threatened them with exposure.

Although she had ceased to be a virgin at thirteen, Judy had been initially attracted by the attentions of this older man whom she met at a local disco. She found his confident lovemaking flattering after the gauche fumblings of her peers and she enjoyed the forbidden excitement of the new sexual experiences he introduced her to, all duly captured, of course, on film.

When these novelties wore off, Benny was able to sustain her enthusiasm by the regular cash payments that accompanied her first forays into 'acting'.

The schoolgirl had been one of his regular 'stars' for a few weeks when she arrived on that Sunday morning at his studio. Himmler Films had informed him that Judy had been chosen to go to London and make a 'special documentary' at Himmler's head office. He had been asked to drive her down.

Judy had never had any aversion to making blue films. She was sophisticated for her years and, far from feeling guilty, she thought the whole thing was fun and she was quite happy to perform with any of the actors that Benny Jackson found for her.

When Jackson told her of Himmler's request, Judy didn't hesitate. The prospect of pursuing a 'glamorous' screen career appealed to her. She pretended to her parents that she was going to stay with a friend in Cornwall for the week, even getting her father to drop her off at the station to add credence to her story.

Instead of catching a train, she walked to Benny Jackson's studio. They spent a few hours making another video before setting off in his Mondeo for the capital.

Benny was not told where Himmler's premises were. He had to drop the girl outside Fortnum and Mason's in Piccadilly where someone would pick her up.

The journey took place in virtual silence because, contrary to Gavin 'Big Ben' Davis's opinion, Judy Whay no longer cared much for Jackson whom she regarded as a bit of a yob.

He, in turn, felt threatened by her independent streak. In fact, of late, he'd often made sure that Judy got the most unpleasant roles in his videos.

But Judy Whay's last visit had unnerved him.

One thing he was not prepared for was her murder.

It was obvious, even to Benny Jackson, that Himmler Films were involved in the crime. And if they were prepared to kill cold-bloodedly, for whatever reason, they would think nothing of doing the same to him if they thought he had betrayed them.

What concerned him most was whether the police would trace the girl back to him. Had anyone seen her in his Mondeo?

He realised he knew nothing at all about Himmler Films other than the box office number. The instructions and cash payments he received bore no address or phone number. But the people at Himmler knew where to find him.

All he could do was wait and hope. He had been careful to remove every piece of evidence of his pornographic activities from his studio and, as each day had gone by, he breathed a little easier.

Until today and the shock visit of the two men from Scotland Yard.

He didn't believe the Inspector's claim about a witness watching him perform with the girl. That was bullshit. The only people in his studio beside the girls were his cronies and they'd all be frightened to talk. They had too much to hide.

But who had given him away?

There had been an actor that Himmler themselves had sent down one week, a fellow called 'Big Ben', but Benny couldn't see it being him. He worked for them for Heaven's sake.

The only other person he could think of was the little guy who ran a video rental shop in Bath. He was the only person who knew of his connection with Himmler Films. Apart, that is, from Judy Whay and she was dead.

No, it had to be Roland Pawson. He'd heard rumours about him having connections with the police. He must get to him first and shut him up for good.

He pulled up his car outside Pawson Video Libraries and marched inside.

It was barely half an hour since Sergeant Prole had called and taken away the Himmler catalogue so Roland Pawson was more than a little nervous at seeing an irate Benny Jackson in front of him.

'Have you had the Law in here?' demanded the visitor.

Pawson's expression was that of a sheep at the door of the abattoir. 'What?'

'I've just had Scotland fucking Yard round my gaff asking questions about that Bath girl what got murdered.'

'Why should it be anything to do with me? I don't know her.'

'You're the only person in these parts dealing in Himmler Films. I bring you a catalogue last night and this morning I get a visit. I don't believe in coincidences.'

Pawson realised his reputation as a 'snout'

had preceded him. 'I rent them out. I don't know anything about what's in them.' He tried to feign ignorance. 'Anyway, what's all that got to do with the Bath girl?'

Jackson ignored the question. 'They're probably on their way now. You'd better shut up shop.'

'You must be joking. I've got a living to make.'

Jackson produced a knife from beneath his coat. 'You heard what I said. We're going for a ride.'

He thrust the knife into Pawson's throat and the shopkeeper jumped back. 'All right, I'll come. Where are we going?'

'You'll find out. We'd better go in your car, they may be looking for mine.' Pawson had a Nissan Micra, a car not built to accommodate a man of Jackson's girth. He squatted uneasily in the front passenger seat. 'Right. Now just drive where I tell you, OK?'

Roland Pawson obeyed but he was a frightened man. He didn't know where they were going and he wasn't sure if he'd get the return trip.

As he drove, he tried to work out how he could escape but blind panic was setting in and he couldn't think straight. Should he drive to the police station and run inside? Could he jump out at traffic lights? If he crashed the car, he might be injured as well as his captor.

One thing seemed certain, the further he drove, the nearer his death loomed.

By now, they were out in the country and approaching a bridge over a disused railway line. There were no people about and no cars in sight.

'Stop at the other side of the bridge,' ordered Jackson, pressing the knife against Pawson's chest.

Roland Pawson knew it was now or never. He wrenched the wheel to one side, pressed the brake and sent the Micra toppling through a flimsy wooden fence and a fifty-foot drop to the derelict sleepers below.

As the dust settled, one man was thrown clear but the other, entangled by his seat belt, was trapped in the car as the fuel tank exploded and within five horrifying minutes he was burnt to an unrecognisable cinder.

24

The team of detectives arrived back at Scotland Yard early on Tuesday evening. There had been no new developments in their absence. Marian Lynch was still missing and, despite numerous 'sightings' by members of the public, neither she nor Colin Vickers had been traced.

'I'll take over the Himmler Films enquiry,' said Robin Knox to Glass, 'and tie it in with the Spa Killings investigations. Give you chance to get this Pantomime Cow business sorted.'

'Not to mention yesterday's bank raid, the jewel robbery in Mayfair and that fellow selling the Big Issue beaten to a pulp in the Tottenham Court Road subway, you mean?' said Glass. 'You can tell the season of goodwill's almost upon us.'

'How's it going, the pantomime case?'

'Nowhere at the moment. We found £500 in used notes in Gregory Oliver's flat that we can't account for. They weren't there after Cadamarteri's death but there's nothing in the bank accounts to show where it came from.'

'What's your guess?'

Glass shrugged his shoulders. 'Could be any one of a number of things; gee-gees, the Lottery, hush money, drugs, you name it. He was a bit old to be a rent boy. I suppose he could have robbed a Post Office.'

'What about the motive?' asked Knox, side-stepping his father-in-law's excursion into whimsy.

'That,' said Detective Chief Inspector Glass, 'is what I intend to find out.'

★ ★ ★

It was in the early hours of Wednesday morning when Colin Vickers' blue Mondeo was discovered in the Birmingham multi-storey car park. An off-duty policeman had chosen the deserted venue for a spot of extra-marital inter-departmental groping with an off-duty policewoman.

He immediately recognised the vehicle as the one the whole country was searching for and, putting duty before desire, he telephoned in his find to headquarters.

The news was relayed to Scotland Yard as Detective Chief Inspector Knox arrived at his desk.

'He could be anywhere,' he said. 'The car

park's next to the station. He must have taken the train.'

'Haven't we got the blue Mondeo already though?' pointed out Sergeant Evans. 'Benny Jackson's car up in Bristol.'

'A thousand to one coincidence that they're both the same make and colour,' replied Knox. 'We know Vickers is involved because we've got his dabs on Marian Lynch's front door key. Once we get forensic onto it, I'm sure we'll find evidence that the girl was in the car.'

'What about the tyre marks where the Buxton girl was killed?'

'Emma Turner, you mean? Yes, they were from a Mondeo too but whether it was Jackson's or Vickers', I wouldn't like to say.'

'You mean there could be more than one killer, sir?'

'More likely that there's more than one Mondeo, Evans. Ford have had a good year or don't you read the Autocar?'

'But if Vickers is on the run, where is the girl?'

It was a reasonable question but one the Chief Inspector was unable to answer. Privately, he was afraid that Marian Lynch was already dead.

'I mean,' continued Evans, 'even if Vickers

has done a runner by rail, he can hardly have abducted the girl on a train.'

'He could have switched cars,' pointed out Knox. 'Anyway, the main priority now is to find Benny Jackson. Get on to Bristol and see if Haydn Prole has had any luck tracing Pawson's car. I also want to go to this sex shop in Soho that Walter Glass called on. They might tell us where Himmler Films are if we lean on them.'

But both avenues of investigation in the end yielded nothing.

When Knox and Evans walked through Berwick Street market and down the passage to the Sex Emporium previously visited by Detective Chief Inspector Glass and Sergeant Moon, they found a statuesque blond behind the counter who swore total ignorance of Himmler Films.

'You don't mind if we look?' smiled Knox, indicating the rows of videos on display.

'Help yourself, luv. Just don't get too excited. I haven't got any cold water handy.'

'I couldn't see Mrs. Evans in one of those,' smiled Knox, pointing to a flimsy diaphanous negligee that barely reached the display model's bottom.

'Oh, I don't know,' said Evans. 'She could probably use it as a hairnet.'

They spent the next ten minutes examining

the credits on the video boxes but the name of Himmler Films was noticeably absent.

'Where's the man that used to be here, the man with the shaven head?' Knox recalled Glass's description.

The blond, who was the wrong side of forty to be wearing a micro skirt, looked puzzled. 'George, you mean? Oh, he's left, luv. Joined a monastery.'

'We're wasting our time,' said Knox, angrily. 'Let's go.'

The bad news from Bristol, when they returned to the Yard, was that Roland Pawson's car was still missing, along with its owner. Pawson's mother, with whom he lived, told the police that he'd left home on Tuesday morning and she'd expected him back at teatime as usual, but he didn't show up. The last person known to have seen him was Sergeant Prole who had called into his Bath shop on Tuesday morning.

'I want Pawson's car found and I want Jackson's Mondeo taken apart,' Knox instructed his West Country counterpart. 'Judy Whay's been in that car and God knows who else. And get back to me like yesterday.'

Another setback for Knox came later in the day when Forensic regretted they were unable to find any evidence of Marian Lynch ever having been in Colin Vickers' blue Mondeo.

'I don't understand it. I'd have put money on Vickers being our man,' he declared. 'We're back to square one. Every time we think there's an opening in this case, the door slams in our faces.'

'Well somebody took Marian Lynch from that lock-up in the Potteries, so, if it wasn't Vickers, who was it?' asked Sergeant Evans.

'Vickers has to be involved somewhere. His prints were on the key, for Christ's sake. He must have switched cars or had an accomplice. Look, get on to Steve Rimmer at Stoke and ask him to speak to that witness again, the burglar. He's the one who said the car was a blue Mondeo. And we'd better check those other two people with blue Mondeos that were staying in the area, the one from Matlock and . . .'

'And the fellow in Bristol,' finished Evans.

'Suddenly we've got a plethora of blue Mondeos, but I think we can safely put Benny Jackson down for the Bristol connection. Prole's men are giving his car a going over and I expect we'll have enough evidence from that to nail him for Judy Whay's abduction . . .'

'I'd take nothing for granted in this case,

sir. I mean, we thought Vickers was cast iron yesterday.'

'Maybe you're right. Check both of them, and the woman while you're at it.'

As the day progressed, things didn't get any better. Enquiries at the Post Office confirmed that the box numbers used by Himmler Films were constantly changing but they were all accommodation addresses and mailboxes that had been rented in various names, usually those of the current England cricket team.

'They're just playing silly beggars with us,' seethed Robin.

'But who are they?' asked Trevor Evans, sagely.

'The people behind Himmler Films, who-ever they are? We've only seen monkeys. I want to know who, and where, are the organ grinders.'

* * *

One of the monkeys to whom Knox referred, although Knox did not know of his existence, was Julian Swift.

He had spent Tuesday and Wednesday as he had spent Monday, filming Marian Lynch in scenes of increasing depravity. Half-conscious with drugs, her body racked with pain from her ordeal, she lay on the bed in the London flat sobbing quietly.

She knew instinctively that these people were going to kill her in the end. In the meantime, she wondered how much more cruel and perverted abuse she could take.

On Wednesday evening, Julian received word that Marian had been chosen for the Special Treatment. He was delighted with the news, which would result in a considerable sum of money for him.

He was even going to help with the production, which pleased him even more, since, from an early age, he had exhibited deviant tendencies bordering on sadism.

In fact, he was quite excited by the possibility that the end of the film would coincide with the death of fifteen year old Marian Lynch.

* * *

Marjorie Ball was a sprightly spinster of seventy-five who lived alone on the outskirts of Bath with her arthritic Jack Russell terrier, Eric. On fine days, she was wont to take the little creature out in her 'C' reg. Metro for a drive in the country, where she would stop the car and let Eric hobble around in a suitable field.

On Wednesday afternoon, she chose one of her favourite routes that led past the old railway line. At one time, the council had had ambitious plans to develop the site, initially for an industrial park and then, when that failed, for residential use.

In the end, nothing got done, the weeds grew, wildlife took over and some bright bureaucrat declared the area to be one of outstanding natural beauty and signs went up proclaiming it to be a designated Country Walk.

Marjorie parked close to the railway bridge and opened the back door for Eric to stumble out. Wagging his apology for a tail, the dog wheezed his way up the bank, stopping only to relieve himself against an old fence.

Marjorie stooped to examine some bluebells and watch the progress of a willow warbler flying close to a nearby hedge. When she turned round, Eric was nowhere to be seen. She called him but to no avail.

Clutching her handbag, she trudged up the slope round the other side of the bridge and saw Eric in the distance chewing what looked to be a bundle of rags. As she came closer, she saw to her horror that the rags enclosed a person.

Having driven for the Red Cross during the War and experienced varying assortments of amputated limbs and splattered carcasses, Marjorie was not squeamish about bodies. She kicked Eric, who was now relieving himself on the person's shoe, to one side and leaned over to gain a better aspect.

The person turned out to be a small, middle-aged man and he was breathing.

Marjorie tore open his coat and began to examine him. His right arm was broken and possibly his pelvis. He had a bad gash to the side of his head which had stopped bleeding but which was probably responsible for his present comatose state.

She didn't hesitate. From her handbag, she pulled out her mobile phone and dialled 999.

Roland Pawson would soon be in safe hands.

It was only then that she saw the burnt out wreck of the Nissan Micra.

25

Wednesday found Detective Chief Inspector Glass back at the theatre with Sergeant Moon. He had arranged for the cast to be present for interview, despite it being a free afternoon for them.

Marsha Flint gave them her usual bright smile but it was superficial. 'You've ruined my afternoon, Chief Inspector. I usually do my Sainsbury's shop on a Wednesday.' She gesticulated to the tall, blond, bronzed beach-boy by her side. 'You don't mind Nigel being here do you? He's my boyfriend over from Sydney.'

Nigel wore an ankle length fur coat, which suggested he was having trouble acclimatising to an English winter. He put a protective arm round Marsha as if to establish his claim on her.

'I won't keep you long,' promised Glass. 'I just wanted to know if Mr. Cadamarteri or Mr. Oliver mentioned winning any large sums of money?'

'Not to my knowledge, they didn't. In fact, I always got the impression they were a bit hard up, that's why they were doing the pantomime.'

'Have you any idea where they used to go when they weren't at the theatre?'

The singer thought for a moment. 'Sometimes, they went to that little bistro in town for the pre-theatre meal. Apart from that, I don't know.'

'Thanks anyway.'

'Have you no idea who killed them yet?' Her expression changed to one of genuine fear. 'You don't really think the rest of us may be in danger do you?'

'Of course not.' Glass smiled reassuringly as they took their leave but he didn't feel so confident. He had no idea why the two actors had been killed. The only thing they had in common was their profession and their sexual persuasion and Marsha Flint shared both proclivities.

Their next call was on Jim Smith. 'I missed a day's work because of this,' he grumbled. 'A voice-over for a petfood advert.' He wore a fur hat of the type Glass remembered being popular in Harold Macmillan's day. With his black, bushy beard and burly gait, The Wicked Baron had the appearance of a Cossack soldier.

'I'm terribly sorry,' apologised Glass insincerely. 'But this is a murder inquiry.'

'What is it this time? I've told you everything I know which is very little.'

'I'm trying to find out what the two gentlemen did in their spare time.'

'Why should I know? I don't mix with poofters.'

'They may have said something in your presence.'

He thought. 'Funnily enough, I did hear the little chap . . . '

'Max Cadamarteri,' supplied Moon.

'Yes. The one that was killed first. I did hear him tell his partner,' Smith showed his obvious disgust at the word's connotations, 'that he'd seen Harry Hooper at this Turkish Baths in Chelsea.'

'I didn't know there was a Turkish Baths in Chelsea.'

'They call them saunas nowadays but it's the same idea isn't it? A load of bloody puffs feeling one another up beneath the steam.'

Sergeant Moon spoke up. 'In our experience, sir, saunas and massage parlours are more usually associated with heterosexual prostitution. That is, of course, those with any criminal element attached. I'm sure that most saunas are highly respectable establishments.'

Glass doubted that but said nothing.

'I've heard of this place before. It's definitely a meeting place for poofs.'

'So the old gentlemen would feel at home there,' said Glass, patronisingly. 'Odd about

250

Hooper though. He's no queer.'

Sergeant Moon, who was politically correct in the extreme, seethed quietly. He hadn't heard the word 'gay' mentioned in any of these conversations.

'Anyway,' said the Wicked Baron, 'you said you wanted to know where they went and I've told you. Can I go now?'

'Of course, sir, and we're very grateful for the information.'

'Surprise, surprise,' murmured Glass to his sergeant. 'So is there a connection between our loveable Cockney comedian and the two victims. I wonder what it is. Let's go and see our Happy Harry.'

'Back again,' Harry Hooper greeted the two detectives with heavy sarcasm. 'Your day off yesterday, was it?'

'We were in Bristol. This isn't the only case we're working on,' said Glass, shortly. 'I'd like to know, sir, where Mr. Cadamarteri and Mr. Oliver spent their spare time when they weren't at the theatre. I thought you might have had some idea.'

Harry Hooper lay back in the leather armchair in his dressing room and took a sip from a glass of gin and tonic. The two policemen had been offered stools but preferred to stand. In place of his customary Alice the Cook costume, the comedian wore

251

an Italian style suit and Glass could see now why women might find him attractive. He had a dark, sallow complexion with an aquiline nose and prominent cheekbones. Moreover, he had an air of authority that had been submerged by his Alice the Cook persona.

'How do I know? I never went anywhere with them.'

'That's strange,' said Glass affably. 'We've been told that you had a meeting with Mr. Cadamarteri at a Turkish Baths in Chelsea.'

Hooper's face reddened. 'It's a lie.'

'You mean, you've never been to the baths or you've never seen Mr. Cadamarteri there?'

'Both. Well, I may have been there once, I'm not sure, but I certainly never saw that man.'

'How odd! because he told Mr. Oliver he'd seen you there.'

'He may well have said he'd seen me, Inspector, but I certainly didn't see him.'

'Chief Inspector,' barked Glass. 'Do you often attend saunas, Mr. Hooper?'

'Occasionally. I'm health conscious. I work-out at the gym and I go jogging.'

Glass had always believed that most of the comedian's jogging was of the horizontal variety but declined to say so.

'So you admit you attended the Turkish Baths . . . '

'I *might* have done.'

' . . . but you never spoke to Mr. Cadamarteri there?'

'That's correct.'

'But he might have seen you there without you knowing?'

'I'd say it was extremely unlikely. He probably mistook someone else for me.'

'Oh, come now, sir, yours must be one of the most recognisable faces in the country.'

'Kind of you to say so.' Hooper looked more like he'd received a personal insult. 'But a lot of people look like me, I've got a thousand doubles.'

Glass changed the subject. 'You mentioned at our last meeting that Mr. Cadamarteri gave you tips for a race. Did he back the horses himself?'

'I don't know. I presume so.'

'Did he ever mention to you any recent big wins shortly before he died?'

'Not that I remember.'

'Only, we found £500 in his possession and we couldn't think where the money had come from.'

'Come to think of it,' said Hooper, 'he did say something about an accumulator he had going. If this horse were to win at Cheltenham later in the week, he'd be in for a tidy packet.'

'And did it win?'

'I've no idea. He never told me what it was. But, if you say you found £500 on him, then it must have done.'

'Thank you for your time, Mr. Hooper. You've been most helpful.'

'I'm sure he's lying,' said Glass as they drove back to Scotland Yard.

'About the horse?' asked Moon.

'And the baths too. He must have been up to something. Why should he go to meet Cadamarteri in the Baths when he can see him at the theatre at any time?'

'Perhaps it was just a chance meeting. Smith only said Cadamarteri had seen Hooper there, not spoken to him. They could have both been there together without realising it, like he said.'

Glass wasn't satisfied. 'In which case, why should Hooper lie about it?'

Sergeant Moon couldn't supply an answer and he was equally puzzled about Hooper's account of the £500 gambling success. 'What about these supposed winnings? Why should he make up a story about an accumulator bet if it wasn't true.'

'I don't know, Moon,' Glass pursed his

lips, 'but I tell you one thing that's curious. That race meeting he mentioned at Cheltenham, Robin Knox would be interested in that. He's dealing with these Spa killings.'

'So?'

'Cheltenham is a spa town.'

26

Sandra Mills was surprised to find two policemen at the door of her Matlock home when she returned from her job in the local estate agents. Sandra was a slim woman in her early forties with short blond hair and a friendly smile.

They showed her their ID and she invited them into the semi-detached house in the upmarket part of the Derbyshire spa town. A small Yorkshire Terrier came out of the lounge to bark at them.

'Quiet, Hector,' she said.

'Does your husband still own a blue Ford Mondeo, ma'am?' The first policeman read out the number.

Sandra was horrified. 'Oh my God, he's not had an accident has he?'

'No, it's all right. Nothing to get alarmed about. It's the car we're after. We're doing a check on all Mondeos, part of an enquiry.'

'I see.' She didn't but she was relieved that her husband was all right.

Not two minutes later, the Mondeo pulled up outside the house. Christopher Mills jumped out, saw the police patrol car and ran inside.

'What's all this?' he asked. He was an athletic man, tall and lean. He wore a tracksuit and trainers.

'Nothing to be alarmed about, sir,' repeated the first policeman. 'It's about your car, that's all.'

'I've not been speeding.'

'Nothing like that. I wonder, can you tell me where you were during these days in March?' He read out the dates from when Emma Turner first went missing to when her body was found on the moors near Buxton, less than half an hour's drive from Matlock.

'I'll have to check my diary. Come through to my study.' He led the officers into a book-lined room where a P.C. stood on a mahogany desk. From the top drawer he removed a desk diary. 'Let me see, yes, I was in Bristol on a course. I'm a physiotherapist at the local sports centre. I visit schools and colleges round the county and every so often, they send us on refresher courses.'

'That's fine, sir. I'll just make a note of where you stayed. Now what about this weekend just gone, between Friday and Sunday?'

'Look what is this? I've a right to know.'

'A blue Mondeo was used in crimes on both these occasions. Consequently, we're carrying out checks to eliminate innocent parties. Last weekend, sir?'

'We went down to Stoke on Trent for the weekend. My daughter's at college there so my wife and I and my other daughter went down for the weekend.'

'And stayed at the Post House?'

'You're well informed.'

'If you don't mind, we'd like Forensic to give your car the once-over. Only take a couple of hours. We'll have it back with you by tomorrow night.'

'You're joking. I need my car for work.'

'This is a murder enquiry, sir. Could you perhaps use your wife's car tomorrow?'

Christopher Mills backed down. 'If you're sure I'll have it tomorrow, though God knows what you'll find in my car.'

What the forensic team did find were tyres that matched the prints left in the wintry mud-caked moors near the Cat and Fiddle and traces of hairs belonging to the murdered sixteen-year-old Buxton shopgirl, Emma Turner.

★ ★ ★

Back in Stoke on Trent, Superintendent Steve Rimmer had Willy Burr brought in for questioning.

'It's about the blue car you saw at the Business Park.'

'So it was a body,' said the young offender triumphantly.

'What makes you say that?'

'You wouldn't have brought me here otherwise. Do I get let off the charges then?'

'How sure are you that it was a Ford Mondeo?'

'I don't have to go into the witness box do I? Look, it was dark and I was right down the road.'

Rimmer passed him a page from a magazine that featured colour pictures of current British cars. 'Tell me what cars these are.'

Burr scrutinised the page. 'An Escort, a Citreon, A Polo and a Fiesta,' he said after much deliberation.

The Superintendent took the paper away. 'That's all I wanted to know,' he said. 'See you in court.'

'So much for our witness,' grumbled Detective Chief Inspector Knox after he came off the phone from Steve Rimmer. 'He couldn't tell a Sherman tank from a bloody Robin Reliant.'

'So it needn't have been a Mondeo that Marian Lynch was taken in?'

'No. It needn't.' Robin Knox looked grim. 'I just wonder where Vickers fits in all this.'

He didn't have to wonder much longer. A phone call came in from a Mr. Andrew North who ran a drug store in Burslem. Mr. North told Knox he had been drinking in a pub in the centre of Hanley on Friday evening when he spotted a salesman who had called on him at his shop earlier that day to show him his range of ladies hygienic products.

The salesman's name was Colin Vickers and he had been calling on Mr. North for several years in his capacity as the area representative for SanDan.

'I've been out of town for a few days and I only saw the picture in the paper today. I recognised Colin immediately.'

'What about the girl?'

'The one that's missing, you mean? Yes, she was in there too but not with Colin. She was with another bloke, a lot younger. They left together. Funnily enough though, she did talk to Colin.'

'Oh yes?' Knox was suddenly interested.

'Yes, it was on her way out. She bumped into him and knocked his drink over.'

'Is that all?'

'Well, I was at the other side of the bar so I couldn't see much but it was all over

260

in a few seconds. Her boyfriend came back and they went out. Colin was still there on his own when I left.'

'Did you see him pass anything to her, or her to him.'

'Oh no, I wasn't that close and they'd both bent down, anyway, to pick up the glass. I suppose they could have done. In fact, now's I think about it, he did seem to hand her something, as if she'd dropped it when she bent down.'

'You didn't see what it was? A key perhaps?'

'No idea. But he didn't look like he knew her at all. It seemed to be just an accident in passing, a quick apology and that was it. She was off with the other bloke.'

'Thank you, Mr. North. You've been most helpful.'

'I hope he's not in any trouble. You don't really think Colin could have anything to do with this girl's disappearance?'

Not any more, thought Knox. He took the man's details and arranged for him to go into the Stoke on Trent police station and help compile an identikit picture of the young man with Marian Lynch. More likely than not, this was the person called J. Smith who rented Monroe Studios at the Business Park.

'It could have been pure chance, then?' said Sergeant Evans, when told of the phone call. 'Vickers could be in the clear after all.'

'Could be.' Robin was reluctant to abandon his chief suspect. He had nobody else to replace him with. He was about to go for a cup of tea and a sandwich in the canteen when intelligence came through from Bristol about the body found in the Micra.

'We're pretty certain it's Benny Jackson,' Sergeant Prole told him, 'but we'll know for sure when we've had the dental records.'

'How's Pawson?'

'Still unconscious but he'll live. A few broken bones. He's lucky. Jackson was toasted.'

'Another suspect gone,' Robin sighed when he replaced the receiver.

'We'll have to find new ones,' said Trevor Evans buoyantly, trying to cheer up his superior.

'God knows where from.'

It was not until the following day that they learnt about Christopher Mills and the third blue Mondeo.

27

'I think I might go to the Valley on Saturday,' said Detective Chief Inspector Glass. It was breakfast time on Thursday morning at the Knox household. 'Charlton are at home to the Rangers.'

'You said you were never going again after last week,' Sue reminded him.

'He's been saying that for years,' laughed Robin, 'and he still goes. It's a form of masochism.'

Glass helped himself to another slice of fried bread and wiped the remains of the tomatoes and egg yolk from his plate. 'They ought to bring back Terry Venables before it's too late and we're in the second division.'

'How's the Pantomime case going?' asked his son-in-law who had little interest in football.

'Coming along,' declared Glass, confidently. 'I'm going along to the Turkish Baths in Chelsea today. Might be some connection. Cadamarteri, one of the victims, used to go there.'

'Take your own towel,' warned Sue, 'you never know what you catch in those places.'

'What about the Himmler business, Robin? Any further on with that?'

'Oh, we've found Benny Jackson.' He recounted the gruesome details of the car wreck.

'At least it'll save on crematorium fees,' said Glass.

'That's awful,' cried his daughter.

'Otherwise nothing.' Robin Knox looked depressed.

'What happened to your big suspect, the one the nation's searching for?'

'Colin Vickers, you mean? It looks like he's been ruled out,' admitted Robin, curtly.

'Ah!' Glass stood up. 'Right then, I'll be getting on. I should be in for tea, all being well.'

'Have a nice day,' smiled Sue, giving her father a peck on the cheek. 'Be careful of young blonde masseuses.'

Glass shuddered at the thought and decided he would ask his widowed friend, Mrs. Lewthwaite, if she would join him for an evening of Whist followed by a hot pot supper at the Compton Road Welfare and Social Club on Saturday night. The anticipation, he thought, would help alleviate the gloom of the football match in the afternoon.

He collected his things and walked to Chiswick High Road and hailed a taxi to take him to Chelsea. He felt lost without his car. The stranded Morris Traveller had been picked up from the M4 and duly repaired by a Bristol garage and would be ready for collection in a week at an estimated cost of £690. Glass wished he'd accepted the Morris Minor Centre offer.

The Turkish Baths were bigger than he had imagined. As well as the bathing area, the building housed saunas, Jacuzzis, and massage rooms.

Glass took out his money and informed the receptionist that he wanted a Turkish bath. He was handed a ticket in return and a white bath towel.

'It's all right,' he explained, handing back the towel and indicating the Tesco's bag he was carrying. 'I've brought my own.'

He followed the signs to the basement and changed in a large room with wooden slatted seats and steel lockers. Bereft of his clothes, the detective did not cut a handsome figure. Years of unhealthy eating combined with a capacious intake of alcohol had caused his body to reassemble itself into a series of large lumps which, deprived of sunshine and fresh air, were of an unflattering off-grey colour.

Clutching his towel, he walked gingerly into the main baths to be met by clouds of scalding hot steam. In the distance, he could see the shadowy figure of the other bathers, many of them, he noted happily, of similar proportion to himself.

He wandered along until he came across an attendant, an effeminate looking man in his late forties. He wore a diamond ring in his left ear.

'Excuse me, you don't happen to know somebody called Max Cadamarteri do you?' He held his towel in front of him coyly like a shield.

The other looked at him suspiciously. 'Who are you?' he asked in a high voice.

'I'm a friend of his,' lied Glass, trying to lisp back in a feeble attempt to gain the man's confidence. 'But I've been away on tour so I haven't seen him for awhile.'

The man's lips trembled. 'You won't know, then. Poor Maxie's dead. He was murdered. It was terrible.' He took out a hanky and blew his nose. 'Terrible.'

'When did it happen?'

'Just over a week ago, that's all. Burglars. Broke into his flat and cut his throat open from ear to ear.' He pulled the side of his hand across his neck to illustrate.

'Who did he used to come here with?'

'On his own mostly. He had a friend, Gregory, but Gregory didn't come down

266

very often. Gregory's dead too.'

'My God!' ejaculated the policeman. 'Not murdered as well?'

'Yes.' There was a pause in which Glass felt they could both end up crying if he wasn't careful. 'The same thing not a week later.'

'When did you last see Maxie?'

'The very weekend before he died. On the Saturday afternoon he came in. I remember because Harry Hooper was in at the same time, you know, from the telly.'

'Was he a regular too?'

'No. Never seen him down here before. I think he'd come to meet someone. The two of them were closeted together for ages in the Jacuzzi.'

'Did you see what the man with him looked like?'

'A big, evil-looking man with shaved head and a scar down his face. Could have played Attila the Hun without make-up.'

Glass thought of where he'd seen someone of that description recently. Of course, the man in the Soho sex emporium, the one called George. He fitted that description

'Did Max mention Hooper to you?'

'I'll say he did. He was chuckling. They were in the same pantomime, you know, *Jack and the Beanstalk*.'

Glass said he did know. 'What was it that made him laugh?'

'I didn't catch it exactly but he was telling me about Hooper being in drag and playing the cook in the show and he muttered something about a snake.'

'A snake?' The Chief Inspector was suddenly alert, causing his towel to slip slightly in his excitement. The drawing of the python he'd found in Gregory Oliver's flat. 'What about a snake?'

'I'm not sure. I think it was a snake but there were some noisy people nearby and I couldn't quite catch it. Whatever it was, it seemed to amuse Max.'

'Did you see him talk to Hooper at all?'

'No. They may have passed one another but, like I say, Hooper was with this other guy. Oh, a right villain he looked too.' He threw up his hands and glanced down at the part of Glass's body no longer covered by the towel. 'You say you're a friend of Maxie's? I've not seen you here before. What's your name?'

'Walter.'

'Hello, Walter. I'm Donny.' He held out his hand and Glass shook it. It was a smooth hand and it hung on to him a full second longer than the policeman would have liked.

'Charming to meet you, Donny,' he smiled though closed lips. 'I'm afraid I shall have to be off now. Matinee, you know. Perhaps we'll meet again.' Hoisting up his towel, he fled to the changing room, threw on his clothes and hurried out of the building to find a cab.

'What do we know about George somebody who works in one of the Soho porn shops off Rupert Street?' he asked, back at Scotland Yard.

'What's he look like?' came the Geordie voice of Detective Inspector Washington.

Glass described him and Washington shook his head. 'Don't know him. Hey, Walter,' he chortled. 'When are you having another of your film shows?' That was a bonny night and no mistake. There were a few ribald laughs and Glass shot the Whitley Bay man a look that would have frozen a furnace.

'Could be George Costello,' piped up Detective Sergeant Snape who, after years in the Porn Squad, knew every racketeer in Soho. 'He's been on the scene for years.'

'Who's he work for?'

Snape grinned. 'George works for whoever pays him the most money. You want a dirty job doing, Costello's your man.'

'Where would I find him when he's not in Soho?'

269

'He used to hang out at Stanistreets Gym near the Elephant and Castle, off the Old Kent Road.'

'Say no more. Thanks, Tom.'

He went along to his office where Sergeant Moon was busy with paperwork.

'There's been a development,' he said. 'Leave that, son, we're off on the trail again.' He recounted his conversation with Donny at the Turkish Baths.

'You've lost me. You say Hooper didn't speak to Cadamarteri? So we haven't got a connection between them.'

'I don't know, we might have. Apparently Maxim was telling some joke to the attendant about Hooper and he mentioned a snake. Remember that drawing?'

Moon, like Robin Knox, had never regarded the python sketch with the same importance that his boss had. 'I can't see the significance.'

Neither could Glass but his intuition told him different. 'There's more. Hooper spent over an hour in the Jacuzzi with that ape we met in Soho last week, the one minding the porn shop.'

'The one whose newspaper you ripped up?'

'That's the one.'

Now the sergeant really was puzzled. 'What

270

would Harry Hooper be doing with someone like him?'

'That, Moon, is what we are off to find out. But first we'll grab some lunch. After an hour in those Baths, I need to put some weight on.'

28

'It's the break we've been waiting for,' said Detective Chief Inspector Knox. The information about Christopher Mills' car had just been relayed to him at Scotland Yard by the Derbyshire police. 'We should have checked out those other three before. It's my fault. I was so sure Vickers was our man.'

'What about the Bristol man?' asked Sergeant Evans.

'Steve Maker? He's clear. He was in Stoke helping his girlfriend who had a stall at some exhibition. She's confirmed it. And before this weekend, he was in Florida for three weeks on holiday so he couldn't have been in Bristol when Judy Whay went missing.'

'How about the fourth Mondeo owner, the woman?'

'She's kosher. Runs a pottery shop in Devon and had come to the Potteries to buy new stock.'

'So, out of the four, it's Mills who's the one after all.'

'Surprising isn't it? Like I say, I'd have put money on Vickers.'

'I wonder why Vickers ran away if he'd

done nothing?' mused Sergeant Evans. 'Steve Rimmer rang his company, you know. SanDan were expecting him to be on the road for them yesterday morning but they've had no word. He's not kept any of his appointments. And we know he abandoned his car. Why?'

'It's obvious,' said Knox. 'His picture in the paper, driving a blue Mondeo, knowing he'd been seen with the girl, his prints on the key and with his record. Christ, no wonder he ran away. Who'd have believed his story? I wouldn't.'

'You're right. I wonder where he is?'

'Could be anywhere. If he's any sense he'd be sipping tequila with Ronnie Biggs in Brazil. He'll come back eventually when we find the real killer and he knows he's in the clear. In the meantime, we could be on the right track with this bloke Mills. Where is he now?'

'They're picking him up now, sir, and taking him to the local station.'

'Good. We'll get a bite to eat in the canteen then drive up there straight away. This could be the big breakthrough, Sergeant.'

Trevor Evans looked doubtful. 'Even if Mills did murder the Buxton girl, he's got an alibi for when Marian Lynch was snatched. And he's a long way from Llandudno where the Welsh girl went missing.'

'On the other hand, there's a Bristol connection. That's where he says he went to this conference.'

'But we know Benny Jackson took Judy Whay.'

'We've no proof on that yet.'

'Oh, sorry, sir, I meant to tell you. Haydn Prole phoned. Bristol forensic came up trumps. Judy Whay was in Jackson's Mondeo all right. No doubt about it. That friend of Judy's, Lois, who saw her in a blue Mondeo, was right.'

'So that's that one sorted.'

'And Pawson may be able to tell us something to confirm it when he comes round.'

'I doubt it. I think it's exactly like that Davis fellow told Walter Glass. Himmler Films have these area managers, as they call them, in different parts of the country who find the girls for them and make the films.'

'So Mills could be the man in Buxton.'

'If he is, Sergeant, let's hope we can hang on to him. Both the area managers we've found so far have ended up dead.'

As he led the way out of his office to the canteen, Knox bumped into his father-in-law in the corridor, coming the opposite way.

'You look in a hurry,' commented Glass. 'Something come up?'

'The girl killed in Buxton, they've traced the car. Trevor Evans and I are going up there now to question the owner.'

'Let's hope you have better luck this time.'

Robin gritted his teeth at the unspoken criticism of his previous endeavours with suspects. 'How did the Turkish Baths go?'

'Quiet,' replied Glass laconically. 'Nothing to get steamed up about.'

The humour was wasted on the younger man. 'Tell Sue I'll be away tonight, would you, Walter?'

'When do you think you'll be back?'

'Providing there's no cock-ups, I should be home by tomorrow teatime.'

Robin Knox should have known better. So far, in the Spa Killings case, there had been nothing but cock-ups.

★ ★ ★

Colin Vickers stayed only three nights at the small Edinburgh hotel. On Monday and Tuesday mornings, he ventured out only as far as the corner store where he bought sandwiches and a can of beer to take back to his room for lunch. Breakfast

275

and evening meals he took in the hotel.

The following day, he bought the local newspaper and searched the accommodation to let adverts. He ticked off three that looked possible and, armed with a street map, walked across town to inspect them.

'I'm sorry, I don't take single gentlemen,' the lady at the first house informed him. 'I've had trouble with them before.'

Colin didn't argue but walked half a mile to the next address. It was an ugly, stone-built, three-storey building divided into numerous apartments and bedsits. The front door was open and smelt of cats. Two of the front bay windows had cracks covered with cardboard.

He carried on walking.

The third address looked more promising. It was the first floor of a semi-detached house and the landlady lived downstairs. She was an attractive divorcee in her late thirties with striking black hair, a voluptuous figure and a face etched with worldly experience.

'The rents £300 a month,' she told him, 'and a month's deposit.' She had a strong Scottish brogue he found fascinating.

'I'm waiting for a cheque to be cashed,' said Colin. 'Can I give you £300 now and the rest at the end of the week?'

He had only four hundred pounds in cash

left and he daren't use his credit cards in case the police traced him. Similarly, he was frightened to ring his mother as, nowadays, calls could so easily be traced.

'I'll trust ye,' smiled the woman and looked straight into his eyes. Colin felt aroused and nervous at the same time and tried to avert his eyes from her white thrusting cleavage.'

'I'm Mrs. Beswick,' she said, holding out her hand, 'but ye can call me Netta.'

'Graham Bradley,' said Colin. He took her hand and felt an electric shock go up his arm.

'I'll be back in an hour with my things,' he said. He returned to the hotel to pay his bill, collected the suitcase and laptop computer, which constituted his only luggage, and took a taxi back to his new digs.

In his room that evening, he imagined what a night would be like with his new landlady. He thought he fancied her even more than the girl in the pub, the girl who'd got him into all this mess. He set about his usual masturbatory activity, his mind on Netta's inviting breasts, when the bedroom door opened and in she walked.

Colin Vickers was covered with confusion and embarrassment but he had no need to be because he was about to experience the most joyful and momentous experience of his life.

'It'd be much more fun if we did it together,' she said softly, reaching out and taking him in her hand. She wore only a thin cotton T-shirt.

Colin couldn't believe it. Unlike Glenys, Netta was a woman who was at ease with sex, happy to talk about, do it and enjoy all its deviations. He had enough self-knowledge to realise that if he'd met Netta at seventeen instead of thirty-seven, his life would have been vastly different.

She wasn't put off by his girlie magazines, in fact she read them with him as they made love. Guided by her gentleness and expertise, Colin's initiation into the delights of sex was the best thing that had ever happened to him.

Afterwards, they cuddled and fell asleep in each other's arms.

The next morning, Netta brought their breakfast up to bed and they resumed their lovemaking from the night before.

'What do you use the computer for?' she asked, during a break in the proceedings when they'd stopped to finish the tea and toast.

He told her about the porn on the Internet and Netta was intrigued and excited rather than disgusted.

'Let's see some then,' she said. Colin

fetched the laptop, switched it on and brought up the Yahoo search engine. Netta watched, fascinated as he typed in the word 'bondage'. She was amazed at how many entries came up.

Colin clicked on one of them and an advert appeared on the screen with an inset picture of a girl wearing a leather peephole bra and carrying a horsewhip in her hand.

'It's just like the movies,' explained Colin, 'you get the sound as well but this is just a trailer. To see the actual films, you have to give your credit card number.'

'And you do this?' asked Netta curiously. Colin confessed he did and Netta felt a warm sympathy for him. Porn was something to add spice to your lovemaking not a substitute for it. She kissed him softly. 'Ye won't have to watch them on your own anymore my sweetheart. Just tell me what you like.'

They lay together peacefully after a second frenetic bout of sex. Netta asked 'Graham' about himself and Colin poured out the whole story. He told her about his shyness with girls, his domineering mother, his job as a salesman and his real name.

'Have ye never had a proper girl friend?' she asked and listened to the story of platonic Glenys. When she asked what he was doing renting a room in Edinburgh when his job was down South, he confessed that he was hiding from the police.

'I once stole some ladies clothes from a washing line,' he admitted. 'I was only seventeen but they keep these things on file.' He told her about the missing Stoke schoolgirl, Marian Lynch, and how he had bumped into her accidentally in the Hanley pub. 'Someone who knew me must have seen me in there, told the police and they put two and two together.'

'And made fifty.'

'With my record, I thought they'd never believe anything I said. I panicked, I suppose.'

'But ye've not done anything?'

'No.'

'And the girl's not been found?'

'No. She could be lying at the bottom of a lake, for all I know and I can't prove I wasn't with her.'

'We'll have to think of something. Ye can't just give up your job and be on the run for the rest of your life.'

Netta turned her attention back to the computer screen on the bedside cabinet which was still flashing a message asking for a credit card number and promising scenes of lascivious and forbidden delight.

'Go on, then,' Netta said. 'Let's see what we get.'

Colin obeyed and typed in the details of his Visa card. On the screen came the picture of a young girl tied to a bedpost. She looked no more than fifteen and she was naked. A man with a shaven head and a scar down his cheek was beating her with a cane and the girl twisted from side to side to avoid the blows, screaming with pain when she was struck on a vulnerable spot.

Netta looked worried. 'It looks very realistic.' Blood was trickling from a small cut on the underside of the girl's right breast. 'You don't think they're really hurting that girl do you?'

But Colin Vickers hardly heard her. He was staring at the screen in horror and disbelief.

The girl on the screen was Marian Lynch.

29

Stanistreet's Gym was in an old brick building near a patch of waste ground that looked like a relic left standing by the German bombers after they had flattened all the houses around it.

They parked the police Escort right outside and Detective Chief Inspector Glass led the way up the iron staircase to the first floor which housed the gym, Detective Sergeant Moon a few steps behind him.

The windows were tiny and barred, letting in little light, but metal lamps hanging from the ceiling sent out yellow beams at regular intervals. Plastered around the walls were old bills, featuring names Glass had never heard of, and peeling black and white photographs of long-ago boxers. Glass recognised Jack Dempsey, Randolph Turpin and Brian London.

About a dozen youths, most of them Afro Caribbean blacks, were hammering punchbags, skipping or pedalling furiously on exercise bicycles. The frantic motion made Glass feel quite tired but it all stopped as the two policemen walked in.

'Can I 'elp you sunshine?' The speaker was about fifty, not a tall man but an exceptionally wide one, his huge girth stretching his dirty striped sweatshirt to bursting.

'Police,' said Glass, flashing his ID card.

'I can see what you are,' snarled the man. Glass wondered what it was about him that so obviously signalled his profession. With his battered trilby, ex-army greatcoat and brogue boots he thought he easily could have passed for an unsuccessful market gardener or maybe a sailor on shore leave.

DS Moon, on the other hand, with his smart black overcoat and earnest expression, was a dead ringer for a Jehovah's Witness. All he needed was a Bible.

'I'm looking for George Costello.'

'Never heard of him.'

The Chief Inspector cast an eye around the building. 'You know, I've made a study of the Health and Safety Act,' he said, conversationally. 'Very interesting piece of legislation the Health and Safety Act, full of peculiar rules. You'd be surprised how many things there are that can get a place closed down, tiny things that you'd never believe, that you'd imagine were quite insignificant. Some of them could even land the proprietor in jail.'

'Whatcher trying to say?' His brain seemed to have difficulty coping with the detective's verbosity. Glass, observing the man's cauliflower ear and broken nose, already had him down for a 'punchie'.

'Only that if you don't tell me where I can find George Costello, sunshine,' he emphasised the word, 'I'll have this apology for Madison Square Gardens shut down by teatime and your boss could find himself in the slammer.'

The ex-bruiser screwed up his face, trying to work out which alternative would bring him the least grief and looking across the gym for assistance. By now, the other inhabitants had resumed their activities and none of them were looking in his direction to help him.

'So what's it to be?' pressed Glass. 'Where's Costello?'

'He ain't here,' he said at last. 'Ain't been in for over a month.'

'Then where will I find him?'

'They say he's doin' a job for a geezer they call Carlos. Up norf.'

'How far north? Birmingham? Liverpool? Glasgow?'

'Nah. Primrose Hill.' The man was obviously not an extensive traveller. 'You wanna watch yourself, guv. This Carlos is supposed to be big time.'

'What's he into?'

'The usual rackets, you know.'

'Whereabouts in Primrose Hill?'

'I've no bleedin' idea. Out of my league all that. It's just what I've heard. But Costello ain't been in 'ere for a month or so. Now piss orf, can't yer. Bad for trade you bein' in 'ere.'

'If we don't find him, we'll be back,' promised Glass.

The two men made their way back to the police car.

'What do you reckon?' Sergeant Moon enquired of his superior. 'You think Costello might have been the one who killed Cadamarteri and Oliver?'

'It's a possibility. He's been known to work as a hit man.'

'You're saying he killed them on the instructions of Harry Hooper?'

'Maybe. Maybe not.'

'But why? Why should Hooper want to kill them?'

'I've not the slightest idea,' confessed the inspector, 'of anything. I'm just going with the flow, as they say, and this is where the current's taking me.'

'I see,' said Moon, who didn't see at all.

'We'll get back to the Yard,' said Glass. 'See if anything's happened there.'

Waiting, thought Moon, for the famous 'Eddie The Nose' to ring. It was a legend at the Yard that Glass relied on informants to solve his cases for him.

As it happened, the Chief Inspector's timing could not have been more propitious. At the very moment he walked into his office, the switchboard phoned through.

'Can you take this call, sir. It's Detective Chief Inspector Knox's case really but he's up in Derbyshire. Somebody called Colin Vickers is on the line from Edinburgh. It's to do with the Spa Killings.'

★ ★ ★

Christopher Mills was brought into the police station in Matlock in a state of angry confusion.

'I don't know what the hell I'm supposed to have done,' he shouted. 'I'm dragged out of my house, brought down here and nobody tells me what's going on.'

'I'll tell you, Mr. Mills,' said Detective Chief Inspector Knox quietly, 'but first let me ask you something. Do you happen to know a young lady called Emma Turner from Buxton.'

'Never heard of her.' The answer was swift.

'You're sure about that?'

'The name doesn't ring a bell. I know a Karen Turner, she's a maths teacher at a school in Matlock. Perhaps she has a daughter, I don't know.'

'This Emma Turner worked in Marks and Spencer in Buxton. She was sixteen years old.'

'Was?'

'She was murdered in March of this year. Strangled. Her body was found on the moors outside the town.'

'Hang on, March? That's why you wanted to know where I was in March. But what's all this got to do with me. Do I look like a murderer? I've never heard of the girl.'

'The reason we first got in touch with you was because we found tyre tracks near the scene of the crime belonging to a blue Ford Mondeo. Last weekend, in Stoke on Trent, another young girl was abducted. We carried out a check of guests with blue Ford Mondeos staying at hotels in the Potteries area and your car number came up.'

'I was with my wife and daughters at the weekend, I've already told the police that at Matlock.'

'I know you have, Mr. Mills, and that

would seem to rule you out of the enquiry except for one small point.'

'And what's that?'

'The tyre tracks on your Mondeo match the ones found near Emma Turner's body and we have found a hair inside the car belonging to the dead girl.'

The colour drained from Mills' face. 'That's impossible.'

'You say you were at a Conference in Bristol at the time Emma Turner was killed. Can you prove that?'

'My name will be on the registration forms, I paid the fee by cheque, I signed the visitor's book. Will that be enough?' Christopher Mills was getting angry again.

'With due respect, sir, you could easily have registered in Bristol, driven back up North, committed the offence and returned to your conference. What we need are names of people who actually saw you there during those days.'

'Fine. That's no problem. I can give you a list of the other delegates. They will confirm I was in Bristol throughout the whole event.'

'If that is the case, Mr Mills, could Emma Turner have been in your car perhaps on another occasion? Have you ever given lifts to hitch-hikers?'

'You're joking. You daren't give lifts to

288

girls nowadays in case they accuse you of rape. Everyone knows that.'

'Have you ever driven the car off road near the Cat and Fiddle pub?'

'No.'

'So can you explain how the vehicle was at the spot where this girl's body was abandoned?'

Christopher Mills looked into Robin Knox's face. 'I can give you one explanation, Chief Inspector. Namely that I was not driving it.'

Knox and Evans exchanged glances. 'What?'

'I went to Bristol in my wife's car that week for the very good reason that my Mondeo was stolen the day before from a car park in Leek. I got it back over a week later. It had been abandoned in Uttoxeter beside the racecourse. And if you lot had had the common sense to ask me that before, you'd have saved yourself the trouble of bringing me down here and wasting both our time. You'll be hearing from my lawyers.'

★ ★ ★

'It's all true, sir,' said Sergeant Evans, glumly. 'I've checked with the records. Mills's car was stolen like he said. They never caught the thieves.'

'No, they wouldn't.' Car theft was so common throughout the country that most forces would be reluctant to waste precious man-hours looking for a thief they'd have little hope of catching. There would be a perfunctory entry in the diary and, one day, some toe-rag would be caught nicking cars, ask for several other similar offences to be taken into consideration and a hundred or so crimes would be transferred like magic into the 'solved' section. Knox knew how it worked.

Besides, Mills had got his car back, hadn't he, so what was the point of doing any more?'

'So Mills and Vickers are both in the clear,' said the sergeant. 'Jackson and Nightingale are brown bread and we're back to square one yet again with not a lead in sight.'

'What about the lad that Mr. North said was with Marian Lynch in that pub? Has his photo been circulated?'

'It has but it's very sketchy and there's been no reaction as yet.'

Knox frowned. 'Somewhere out there are a string of these bloody Himmler area managers and the one I want is J. Smith. He's the one who's taken Marian Lynch. I'm just afraid we might be too late to save her.'

30

'Ye'll have to ring the police and tell them.' Netta told Colin Vickers after he'd revealed to her the identity of the girl on the Internet. They'd finally got out of bed, showered and had a late lunch. Now they were in her downstairs living room discussing the next move and Netta was adamant. 'Apart from getting you off the hook, it could save this girl's life.'

'But they'll know I've been logging on to all the porn channels.'

'So what? Most coppers love all that stuff.' Netta had had a certain experience of the breed and nothing they did would have surprised her. In her less affluent youth, she had been on the game in Glasgow and some of her best clients had been serving members of Her Majesty's police force.

It was not something she was prepared to admit to Colin at the moment, though she would do eventually, but what she knew about the sexual behaviour of policemen would have amazed him. For all his interest in porn and sex, Colin was really quite naive.

'So you think I should tell them?'

'Yes I do, love. Put the television on Ceefax, it'll give you the number to ring if ye have any information.'

Colin felt a great sense of belonging and security in Netta's home and he was instinctively prepared to trust her judgement. He dialled the number on the TV screen.

Detective Chief Inspector Glass listened carefully to what Colin Vickers told him over the telephone, how he had met the missing girl in the Hanley pub and been mistaken for her abductor.

'Why didn't you contact us in the first place?' he demanded.

'I was frightened. I've watched that *Cracker* on television and I knew my record and everything would go against me. You might not have believed me.'

Glass muttered a silent curse to the criminal profiling movement, which he put on a par with other modern phenomena like feminism, counselling and political correctness, all institutions that he would abolish if he ever became Prime Minister.

'So why have you rung now?'

'I've just seen the girl on the Internet, Marian Lynch.'

'What?'

Vickers started to explain about the

Internet site but Glass stopped him. As he had never mastered video recorders or SLR cameras, the detective had no chance of understanding the complexity of computers.

'Just a moment,' he said, 'I'll pass you on to my Sergeant and you can explain to him.'

Unsurprisingly for a man of introspective nature, DS Moon was well versed in computers and was able to follow Colin Vickers' directions with ease.

'Give me your number in case we need to contact you, Mr. Vickers,' demanded Glass when the phone was handed back to him. 'In the meantime, I suggest you get in touch with your company before you lose your job.'

Glass replaced the receiver and turned to his companion. 'Did you get all that?' Moon nodded. 'Can you get it on one of our machines?'

'No problem, sir. So long as it's one with a modem.'

'Right. Let's go.'

They found a suitable computer and Moon brought up the search engine and typed in 'bondage'. The list of entries came up and he brought the mouse down until he found the one Vickers had used. He clicked twice and on the screen flashed the picture of the girl with the whip.

Glass watched in astonishment.

The advert came on offering more delights in exchange for a credit card number. 'Whose credit card should I use?' Moon asked, knowing what the reply would be.

'Use yours, of course, Sergeant. We'll reimburse you.'

'I was just a bit worried about this appearing on some record somewhere. Look what happened to Gary Glitter.'

'Oh, rubbish. I'll say I sanctioned it.'

Moon was unconvinced but, as no alternative presented itself, he went ahead and typed in his credit card number. Almost immediately on the screen came the film of Marian Lynch that Colin Vickers and Netta had watched in Edinburgh.

By now, several of the officers in the adjoining rooms had come in, sensing something important was happening. The atmosphere was tense. There was none of the hilarity of the Christmas party of the previous week.

'Is this live like television or a film?' he asked Moon.

'This will be a video, sir. But they do offer an interactive alternative for more money.'

'What the hell's that?'

'Basically, a camera set up in the room where the girl is. They will ask you what you want to happen next and, if you pay enough money, they'll carry out your wishes. It's the modern way of prostitution.'

Glass was astounded at the sergeant's knowledge. He had always thought of Moon as strangely old-fashioned. 'But they never meet each other.'

'No. So there's no fear of AIDS, nobody gets arrested for kerb crawling or running a brothel. The girls can run the operation from home without fear of another Jack the Ripper or Peter Sutcliffe doing them in and they don't have to hand over half their earnings to pimps.'

Glass was flabbergasted. 'You sound like a salesman, Moon, for computer sex. The condom firms could go out of business if this catches on. Hang on a minute though,' he said, suddenly serious again. 'You say you give instructions to these people. Well, that's OK when it's just the girls doing it on their own but, in this case, Marian Lynch isn't a willing participant. What happens then?'

Moon looked grave. 'That's the danger, sir. If someone pays enough money, these people will do anything to that girl that they're asked to. It's like a menu in a takeaway but in this case, a takeaway of torture.'

'Oh my God.' Glass covered his head with

his hands. He remembered what Robin Knox had told him about the injuries suffered by the victims of the Spa Killer. 'What you are saying is, some depraved nutter with enough money could order Marian Lynch to be mutilated on screen just to give him kicks.'

'Worse than that, sir. Remember what happened to those other three girls. There are a lot of crazy people out there. How much, I wonder, would they pay to have Marian Lynch killed?'

'If she isn't already dead. You say this is a film? How can we get the live version.'

Moon clicked back to the index. 'More money,' he said and entered his credit card details again.

A metallic voice came through the speakers. 'We want three more people to pledge ten thousand pounds and we will circumcise the girl. We have seven already, we need just three more.'

The screen was filled with a picture of Marian Lynch, lying on the same bed, covered in bruises and in a distressed state of semi-consciousness.

Next to the bed sat a shaven headed man with a scar down one cheek and wearing a pair of headphones.

'George Costello,' breathed Glass.

'He's probably listening for instructions in those headphones,' said Moon.

As he spoke, Costello stood up, held up the cane in his right hand and brought in down on the girl's body. She whimpered as it hit her.

Glass cried out. 'My God,' he said. 'And they've abolished capital punishment.'

'At least she's still alive.'

'Get Robin Knox on his mobile. We need him down here.'

Detective Chief Inspector Knox and Sergeant Evans were already on their way back down the M1 from Derbyshire when they took the call.

Knox paled when he heard the news. 'We'll be back in an hour,' he told Glass. 'But what can we do? They could be anywhere in the country. In the world for that matter.'

'I don't think so, I think they're somewhere near. My bet,' he stated, 'would be Primrose Hill.' He didn't go into his reasons.

Sergeant Moon interrupted. 'I don't think we've got much time, sir. Look.' On the screen had flashed up the number eight. 'Yes, the eighth person,' came the metallic voice. 'Only two to go before this girl is circumcised.'

'Who's speaking?' asked Glass.

297

'My guess is a tape recorder, a pre-recorded message. They've put it through some digital devise to disguise the voice.'

On the bed, the girl squirmed. 'She can hear him,' exploded Glass. 'She must be terrified.'

'Something's happening,' said Moon. The camera panned round the room to record the entry of a third person. He came through the door dressed like a Georgian dandy with a golden brocade frock coat, pink breeches and a grey powdered wig. An ornate, brightly coloured silk fan shielded his face from the lens as he walked over to the girl on the bed.

The policemen watched in fascination as he turned his face away from the camera, put down the fan and slowly unfastened his breeches to reveal his erect organ which he guided towards Marian Lynch's tear-stained face.

Glass could hardly believe what he was seeing.

Along the side of the man's penis was a tattoo of a python . . .

The exact replica of the drawing found in Gregory Oliver's flat.

31

'It's the snake,' breathed Sergeant Moon, incredulously, as the camera moved to longshot to take in the whole of the room.

'I knew that was important,' crowed Glass. 'Robin wouldn't believe me.'

'Why did Max Cadamarteri do a drawing of it?' but the Inspector's eyes were on the screen . . .

'Watch,' he snapped. 'That window in the corner, quickly, what can you see through it?'

Moon concentrated his gaze. 'It looks like a mosque through those trees. Oh, it's gone now.' The camera had moved back to close up as the Mozart-like figure leaned over the girl on the bed and concentrated on the rhythmic movements of the snake.

'Wait till it comes back.' After half a minute, the camera panned back round the room and the window came into view again.

'Regents Park,' shouted Glass, 'that's where that building is, somewhere on the edge of Regents Park. Someone find an Ordnance Map. And get together three cars.' He was barking the orders out now. 'We're going in to get these bastards. I want everybody tooled up, we'll take the riot van and tear gas and if anyone tries to escape, shoot them. Oh, and we'll need and ambulance and paramedics for the girl.'

'And for George Costello,' thought Sergeant Moon, who didn't fancy the criminal's chances when he came face to face with Glass.

By the time Robin Knox and Trevor Evans returned, the team was all set to go. Glass had studied the map and decided he knew where the girl was being held.

'I hope you're right,' said Robin. 'We don't want to break into the wrong house.'

'I've worked out the angles. It's got to be this one,' he pointed to a detached mansion marked on the Ordnance sheet. 'Anyway, we've got to take a chance. There's a girl's life at stake and we haven't got much time. Let's go.'

★ ★ ★

Julian Swift sat in the kitchen in the house on Regents Park in some disquiet. He had been here for four days now, ever since he had brought Marian Lynch down from the Potteries for the Special Treatment, and he

300

had become increasingly perturbed about the whole situation.

He had been quite happy to take explicit photographs and videos of the young school-girl, even when she was initially unwilling to perform with other people, and the excessive amount of money he was being paid helped assuage the guilt he felt when the 'actors' began hurting and abusing her.

But now it had gone too far. The last time he had taken her in some food, he had been shocked at her condition but he didn't know what he could do to save her. He was as frightened of these people as she was, especially the shaven headed monster they called George. Julian was not a fanciful person but he had looked into George Costello's eyes and seen The Devil.

A few minutes ago, another person had come to the house, giving the three secret rings on the doorbell for Costello to let him in. Julian had glimpsed him through the window, hidden in a coat and hood, and thought the man's walk seemed oddly familiar, although he couldn't put a name to him.

The stranger had only stayed a short time, now Julian was on his own again with Costello, the cameraman and the girl. The 'actors' who'd been with them earlier in the week to take part in the ever more perverted filming, had now gone.

Julian could sense that something was going to happen but he didn't know what it was. He went back up to the bedroom and opened the door slowly. George was next to the bed operating a tape recorder.

Julian heard this metallic voice announce that a ninth person had signed up. 'Only one person more and this girl will be circumcised on screen for you specially chosen ten people in the whole world to watch. Will she live through her ordeal? We shall soon see.'

George switched off the machine when he saw Julian come in. 'No-one told you to come in here.'

Julian stood almost rigid with shock. 'You're not really going to do that to her.'

'What business is it of yours?' And George leapt up from the bed, grabbed Julian by the jacket and hurled him against the far wall. As he tried to struggle up, a blow from the man's fist sent him crashing unconscious to the floor.

The cameraman, operating the controls from a dressing room adjoining the bedroom, looked on with disinterest. One of Costello's hired hands, he was being paid to do a job, he couldn't care less what was going on around him.

George Costello resumed his position. From next to the bed he picked up a pair of headphones and put them on. Through these he received his instructions. If somebody in Oklahoma or India or Australia made a credit card donation, the information would be relayed to Costello and he would rise from his chair and impose on Marian whatever 'action' the client requested.

When ten people had pledged a thousand pounds each, Carlos himself, the Snakeman, would return and perform the ultimate horror, the removal of the clitoris.

Himmler Films had been the most successful operation George Costello had been involved in. The boss of the operation was a shadowy figure known as Carlos. Costello had never met him. He received his instructions by telephone and his pay by cash in registered packets, half before and half after each job.

His first job for Carlos had been to kill David Osbourne, a task he had carried out speedily and efficiently. He had moved around the porn industry, keeping his ears open for information to relay back to his boss and several times he had taken part in Himmler's videos, sating his appetite for cruelty.

It was back in March that Carlos had

started his plan for murder on the internet. Emma Turner had been the first victim, netting Carlos fifty thousand pounds of which Costello received twenty per-cent for disposing of the body, using a blue Mondeo he had stolen from Matlock for the purpose.

It was there, in Buxton, that a man claiming to be a friend of Carlos first showed up to take part in filming. He arrived in full drag, dressed as a pantomime dame and took part in the final horrific reels with Emma Turner. The only thing Costello really noticed about him was his startling python tattoo.

Maxine Berry had been the second victim, in Llandudno. They had taken the camera up there and filmed her in an industrial unit near Colwyn Bay which their Welsh area manager, one Ray Wright, had rented for them. When they'd finished, she'd been left to burn, along with the lock-up. The take had gone up to sixty grand.

Carlos must have had some dispute with Mr. Wright, however, because Costello had to arrange an unfortunate boating accident for him. Possibly due to the weights securing his legs, the Welshman still hadn't surfaced months later and, strangely, nobody had reported him missing. Carlos merely concluded he couldn't have been very popular.

Once again, the mysterious stranger appeared at the shoot, this time in the guise of a Chinese mandarin. He must have enjoyed the experience because he turned up again for the next film, shot in this very house with the Bath schoolgirl, Judy Whay. On this occasion, he had dressed up as Robin Hood and again Costello was treated to a sight of the python although he had never seen the man's face.

In every film, this man participated in the worse of the atrocities.

Now he had been here in the house again tonight, resplendent in a powdered wig like an eighteenth century fop, administering pain and suffering to Marian Lynch.

George Costello did not know it but this was the very man he knew as Carlos, the mysterious figure behind Himmler Films.

A voice came in his cans. 'It's getting late. That's it for tonight. We'll finish it off tomorrow morning. We might get an extra couple of grand in.' The caller disconnected.

Because he had the headphones on, Costello didn't hear the front door open, or the stifled footsteps of the policemen searching the floor below.

Nor did he hear them on the staircase as

they approached the bedroom where Marian Lynch had been a prisoner for nearly ninety-six hours.

The first intimation George Costello had that something was wrong was when Detective Chief Inspector Walter Glass burst through the door, followed by three armed officers. Before Costello could move, the policeman smashed the side of his gun against the gangster's nose, splintering the bone into smithereens.

Glass turned towards the camera. 'And that, my perverted friends, is the end of the show for you.' And he put his size twelve boot through the lens, causing extensive damage to the face of the cameraman in the room behind.

★ ★ ★

'Only three people in the house,' said Knox, as the army of policemen and equipment returned to Scotland Yard.

'How many more do you need?' asked Glass. 'It's hardly M.G.M.'

Marian Lynch had been taken to hospital, accompanied by W.P.C. Wendy Ngooma. Her parents had been notified of her safety. Early examinations suggested she had suffered no lasting damage although the bruises would take some time to heal.

Julian Swift, on recovering consciousness, was charged and taken into custody. It was expected he would serve a long prison sentence.

'They'll love him in the Scrubs,' remarked Glass. 'He probably won't be able to walk straight for two years after he comes out.'

'All that's left is the Snakeman,' declared Robin. 'Likes to appear in his own films, doesn't he? A bit like Hitchcock.'

'I thought this was it,' said Sergeant Evans. He was looking decidedly off-colour. The realisation that it could have been Linzi Pennington, his goddaughter, in Marian Lynch's place had obviously affected him. The scenes in the film 'Playground Pets' that he saw at the police party would haunt him forever.

'Oh no. We still want the top man,' said Glass, 'and I know just where he'll be. Robin, come along with us, you too Trevor, and we'll go along and arrest your Mr. Snakeman.

'Where are we going?'

'We're off for a night at the pantomime,' said Glass, almost jauntily. 'This is where all this began. I shall introduce you to the star of Jack and the Beanstalk, in his role as Alice the Cook, none other than the people's favourite comedian, Harry Hooper.' His voice took on a hard note. 'Alias the Snakeman, also known as Carlos and the head of Himmler Films.'

32

Robin Knox looked doubtful. 'We can hardly arrest him there. We'll have to wait till he leaves.'

'No,' interrupted Glass, firmly. 'We can't afford to take any chances. I'm taking him in the theatre. I want all the entrances covered.'

The policemen arrived at the theatre halfway through the second act as Harry Hooper was in the middle of his singing spot.

'He's got some bloody nerve,' remarked Sergeant Evans. 'Coming straight from abusing that kid, onto the stage here.'

Glass flashed his warrant card at the stage door and they trooped backstage. The Chief Inspector sought out Daniel, the ASM, and put him in the picture. 'I've straightened it with the director,' he said, and he outlined his eccentric plan. 'This will ensure the arrest goes ahead with the least possible fuss.'

'I suppose it'll be all right,' the youth stammered, his nervous twitch betraying his suspicions that it wouldn't.

Glass marched to the side of the stage

where members of the cast were waiting for their next call and made straight for the pantomime cow.

'He tapped the front of the cow and spoke a few words in its ear. Daniel stepped forward to unfasten the costume and two slimly built youths stepped out, younger versions of Max Cadamarteri and Gregory Oliver.

Daniel explained to them the scheme and they smiled with amusement.

'A little idea of mine.' Glass explained to his son-in-law who looked bemused at the exchange. 'If Hooper sees two men approaching him looking like coppers, as we do, then there's every chance he'll scarper. This way, we'll catch him unawares.' He held open the costume. 'I'll get in the front. You're in the back, Moon.'

Totally bemused, Moon stumbled into the hind legs and adjusted the furry material round his shoulders.

On the stage, Harry Hooper was launching into a bossa nova rendition of 'Spanish Eyes'.

Glass stepped into the front half of the cow. 'I walk upright and you crouch down to make the body,' instructed Glass as if he had been preparing for this great theatrical moment all his life. 'Right, Daniel, you fasten us in. It's only Velcro so it'll be easy to rip off when we arrest him.'

The ASM moved forward and secured the costume round the two men. 'You're not going out there to do it?' gasped Moon in horror from the back of the costume, but even as he spoke the words he knew the answer.

In the middle of the stage, Harry Hooper, the loveable Cockney comedian and sadistic serial killer, was coming to the end of his song. As the applause died down, he started to tell a joke.

Glass placed the cow's head over his own and attached it carefully to the neck of the costume. His voice came out muffled. 'Robin, you get round the other side in case he makes a dash for it that way. Are the other men stationed at the exits?'

'Yes, sir.'

'Right. Then if you're ready sergeant, let's go.'

'And the Scotsman said, 'what happens if she's not wearing any?' whereupon the Irishman . . . ' The audience tittered as they anticipated the end of Harry Hooper's gag but they were destined never to hear it for on to the stage shambled the black and white pantomime cow, swaying unsteadily from side to side.

Hooper turned to look as the titters turned to laughter and the audience's attention was directed away from him. When he saw the cow his mouth fell open and a puzzled look crossed his face. This wasn't in the script.

The cow came closer until it's head was inches away from his face and a voice very like Gregory Oliver's whispered into his ear. 'It's Maxie and me, Harry. We've come back from the dead to haunt you,' and the creature gave a hideous cackle that froze the blood in Hooper's veins and turned his expression from bewilderment to horror and fear.

Before he could move, Glass ripped open the costume, threw off the cow's head and stepped forward with a pair of handcuffs.

'Harry Hooper, I am Detective Chief Inspector Glass from the Metropolitan Police and I'm arresting you for the murder of Julie Whay among others.' The audience sat in silent amazement, not sure whether this was for real or an unexpected departure into surrealism. 'I must warn you that . . . '

As he was speaking, Glass reached out to attach the handcuffs whereupon Hooper tried to dart away. Quickly, Glass moved forward. The comedian was caught off balance and a nudge from Glass's ample stomach sent him crashing into the orchestra pit below.

It was a long drop and, unluckily for

Hooper, his right leg was twisted sideways by a collision with the grand piano on the way down, resulting in a double fracture of his fibula to add to a broken jaw and severe concussion.

The orchestra leader was the first to collect his wits. 'Start up Marsha's music,' he instructed the band as a mass of police officers ran down the aisles to rescue the unconscious fallen figure of the denounced household favourite.

The audience watched bemused as Detective Chief Inspector Glass, resisting the temptation to launch into his own version of Marsha Flint's recent hit, helped Sergeant Moon out of the pantomime costume where he'd got tangled up in the tail and made a triumphant exit from the stage.

33

After he'd spoken to Detective Chief Inspector Glass, Colin Vickers made a second phone call, to his Sales Manager at SanDan.

He apologised for his absence over the last four days and explained how he'd been the innocent victim of mistaken identity.

His boss listened to the excuses but his mind was already made up. He'd read the newspapers and considered his employee had been the victim of a grave injustice. He didn't want to lose a salesman with Vickers' record. What were a few days absence after years of good service?

'Don't worry about a thing,' he assured him. 'Take the rest of the week off and start again on Monday.'

But Colin had another request. 'Have you appointed a replacement for Adrian Magson yet?' he asked. Magson was one of the star performers in the sales team but was emigrating to Australia and had recently given in his notice.

'The advert's going in this week. Why?'

'I'd like a transfer to his area.'

'What? To Scotland?'

'Yes. I'm getting married and my fiancée and I are going to live in Edinburgh.'

'Why, that's wonderful, Colin.' The sales manager thought it would be the making of him. The lad had been living with his mother for far too long. 'Who's the lucky lady?'

'Her names Netta.' Colin explained how they had met. 'I know it's a bit sudden,' he said.

'Love at first sight, eh?'

Colin blushed on the other end of the phone. 'Something like that.'

'Is your mother pleased?'

'I haven't told her yet.'

There was plenty of time for that, thought Colin. He'd rung her to say he was safe and well and that he would be staying up in Scotland for a few days. Perhaps it might be better to break the news to her after the ceremony. They'd applied for a special licence.

By the following week, Colin and Netta Vickers would be happily married in their Edinburgh home.

★ ★ ★

Roland Pawson, lying in his bed in a Bristol hospital, was relieved to learn that he was no longer in any danger from Benny Jackson, his passenger not having survived the nightmare car journey from which he, himself, had been lucky to survive . . .

Upon his release, Roland decided to concentrate on Disney videos. He heard no more from Himmler Films and found out later that the company had suddenly gone out of business.

Perry Jackson shut his studio upon the tragic death of his only son. There being nobody to carry on the business, he and his wife sold up and retired to the Algarve.

In Bath, Judy Whay's father set up a trust fund at his University to be called The Judy Whay Memorial Scholarship to offer one place a year to a disadvantaged student.

Marian Lynch became engaged to her boyfriend, Mark Peters, and went on to successfully pass her GCSE exams. She was given counselling to help recover from her ordeal.

Harry Hooper broke down after intensive questioning in prison and revealed the whereabouts of the records he had kept of all the personnel who worked for Himmler Films.

A nation-wide police manoeuvre, code-named Operation Lolita, resulted in the arrest of every one of the Himmler 'area managers', all of whom received custodial sentences.

George Costello got life.

Hooper also got life but in his case it was a short sentence. Three days after his incarceration into a secure unit at Parkhurst, four other prisoners forced an iron hacksaw down his throat and he died in agony in the prison hospital twenty four hours later.

34

'We didn't know it at the time,' declared Detective Chief Inspector Glass, 'but all three cases were tied together.'

It was the following evening in the Knox household and Robin, his wife and father-in-law were coming to the end of dinner. Sue had prepared a huge meal of roast duckling, Christmas pudding and champagne.

'Himmler Films was Hooper's own baby,' Glass continued. 'He ran it from the start. Originally, they were churning out run-of-the-mill hardcore stuff for the dirty bookshop market.'

'Are those the ones with the loud music on the sound track and couples at it like rabbits?' enquired Sue innocently.

'They're the ones. No story line, no dialogue and they never do it in time to the music.'

'Give me *Coronation Street* any day. I'm surprised people can be bothered to watch them'

'But they do,' said Knox. 'And the trouble is they become hooked. Porn is no different than gambling, drink and drugs, the more you get, the more you want.'

'He's right,' agreed Glass. 'That's why they should never legalise cannabis. Once it's okay to smoke a few joints, then the temptation is there to move on to something stronger and where do you stop?'

His son-in-law nodded. 'And it's the same with pornography. Once people get used to the straight stuff, they go looking for the bizarre.'

'In my day, the sight of a suspender in *Spick and Span* could keep you aroused for days. There were no Page Three girls then. There was a poem about it, you know; *You never see a nipple in the Daily Express* by John Cooper Clark.'

'And the bizarre,' continued Knox, ignoring his father-in-law's reminiscences, 'means the forbidden. Under age girls, animals and sado masochism.'

'Charming,' said Sue. 'Just as we're eating. Anyone for more rum sauce?'

'And that's what Hooper went for and he was clever about it. He advertised for people to send in their amateur films.'

'And you'd be amazed,' broke in Glass again, 'how many people do. Hundreds of them. I've seen them. It seems like half the bleeding country can't wait to rip each others kit off and get down to it in front of the camcorder, however senile, bloated and deformed they are and despite the fact they're laying themselves open to blackmail.'

'Except Hooper didn't take the blackmail route,' said Robin. 'He went all out for the porn market. The operation was a bit like pyramid selling. He recruited people to recruit more people to send in films and they all got a cut along the way and it became difficult to trace the people at the top.'

'Nobody knew the people at the top,' said Glass. 'It was all box numbers and accommodation addresses at that stage.'

'But when the really heavy stuff came in, Hooper started to get involved. He couldn't help himself. Basically he's a sadist. He got his kicks from torturing people to death. Put him up there with Brady and Hindley and the Wests.'

'He looked so friendly on television too,' sighed Sue. 'You can't believe someone in his position could do all that and get away with it.'

'That's precisely why,' pointed out her father. 'It's like Hughie Green and Robert Maxwell, fame acts as a shield for them. By the way, Robin, have you seen your friend Otis lately?'

'Okay, okay, so he was a bit off beam on this one.'

'Off beam? Off the wall's more like it. I ask you. A series of crimes the magnitude of this and he seriously suspects a lonely sanitary towel salesman living with his mother in Stoke.'

'Stratford on Avon, actually. He had got a record for sex crimes though.'

'Indecent exposure was it? Probably went for a pee in the park and an old lady with binoculars saw him from her bedroom half a mile away and reported him.'

'Knickers from clothes lines, actually.'

'Oh. A job for the Serious Crime Squad.'

'So how did Hooper do it exactly?' broke in Sue before the barter became heated.

'Easy,' said her father. 'Once he'd sussed out the young girls who were prepared to do the bondage films, he went along as the actor, in disguise of course, and, as we now know, ended up maiming and killing three of them on film.'

'And on-line.' Robin looked serious. 'God knows how many people across the globe were paying to watch those poor girls die and we'll never know who they are.'

'I wouldn't be too sure,' said Glass. 'We can check all credit card payments to Himmler Films and whatever other names they go under.'

'The awful thing is, as soon as we catch

one murdering sadist like Hooper, others will be setting up their sites on the Internet. You're talking a potential multi-million pound business.'

They all looked depressed at the thought and Glass quietly wished that Harry Hooper had broken his neck rather than his leg.

'You could say Trevor Evans' goddaughter had a lucky escape,' said Robin. 'She could have been next.'

Sue shivered. 'To think people would pay money to see such things. It doesn't bear thinking about.'

'There's evil in everyone, Sue and if you feed the evil, it grows. Look at all the nice ordinary Germans who joined the Nazis.

'And it'll get worse unless we can find some way of controlling the Internet. Little kids safe at home in their own bedrooms have access to scenes of degradation that a hundred years ago you'd have had to travel to Tangiers to witness.'

'And you can't tell me it won't affect them whatever the social workers might say.' In the overall scheme of things, Glass rated social workers on a par with carriers of bubonic plague. 'It's like the violent computer games. They become inured to it and they want more and half of them can't distinguish the games from reality.' He sighed. 'And to think in my day, we got our excitement from a Rupert annual and a game of 'Owsthat'.'

'Why did Hooper kill the two men in the pantomime cow?' broke in Sue quickly, recognising the onset of one of her father's nostalgia monologues.

'Nice title for a book that, 'two men in a cow', a bit like *Three men in a boat*.' Glass smiled to himself.

'What happened was, Max Cadamateri was at a party where someone was showing one of the Himmler films with Harry Hooper in it. Hooper was unrecognisable in his mask and Robin Hood costume but Max couldn't help but notice his tattoo. It was on the only part of his body exposed in the film. His dick.'

Sue winced. 'Ooh. That must have been painful for him, that needle going in. Can't be many people have a tattoo there.'

'Oh, I don't know,' said Glass wickedly. 'I knew a fellow who had his done. Everyone thought it said 'Ludo' but when the chorus girls came on, it changed to Llandudno.'

'Boom boom,' they guffawed in chorus.

'The old ones are the best,' laughed Robin and refilled all their glasses with champagne.

'Anyway,' continued Glass, 'one day Max comes across Hooper by chance in the Turkish Baths. They're both undressed, of course, and Max recognises the snake and realises it must have been Hooper in the film he'd seen.'

'So Max tried to blackmail him then?'

'I don't think so. He wasn't the type. I think, rather, he teased him about it and Hooper got frightened he might say something. He knew what gossips the two old poofters were and he couldn't risk any scandal of that sort so he went round and offered him money to shut him up.'

'The five hundred pounds.'

'Precisely. But then, Max must have made some little joke and Hooper realised that he couldn't rely on him to keep his mouth shut so he . . .'

'Shut it for him.'

'Exactly. Hooper went round to the flat, slit his throat whilst he slept and went straight out again. Nobody saw him and he wore a scarf round his face, ostensibly to keep out the cold.'

'Why kill Gregory?'

'He couldn't be sure Max hadn't told Gregory. He'd tried a couple of times to arrange accidents and when they didn't work, he took a chance and went round to do a repeat job. He didn't know that Max had made a sketch of his tattoo which, of course, we found.'

Robin Knox finished his drink. 'So that's

five murders all tied up in one glorious night. One of us should get promotion if there's any justice.'

'If there was any justice,' said Glass quietly, 'Hooper would be swinging at the end of the rope. It's at times like this you wish our old friend Timothy Slade was around.' He referred to the notorious criminal of earlier years who had made a practice of killing criminals that he felt had escaped justice.

'Ah yes, The Executioner. Well, you can console yourself that Hooper will have a pretty hard time in jail. There's nothing the other prisoners like better than torturing a child killer.'

'Yes, it's justice of a sort, isn't it? Poetic justice. Hooper's company will have made half the porn that circulates in the cells. All those dirty pictures getting them worked up and they end up taking all their frustrations out on Hooper himself. I like it.'

And Detective Chief Inspector Glass smiled as he drained the last of his champagne.

'Any plans for New Years Eve?' asked Robin. 'I'd heard you might be organising a party again for the police social club.'

'After the last one, you must be joking.'

'Think of it, if you hadn't shown that *Playground Pets* film, we might never have solved this case. Certainly not this quickly.'

'And in time for Rangers match tomorrow.' Not to mention, he thought, his evening with Mrs. Lewthwaite. With a bit of luck, she would invite him to stay the night at her house, which was within walking distance of the Compton Road Welfare and Social Club.

'Why don't we have a family party and see the New Year in at home?' suggested Sue. 'Both of you must have enough time off coming to you and it is going to be a special year with the baby due. Your first grandchild,' she added to Glass. 'Jessica.'

'Do you mind,' said Robin. 'It's going to be a boy. Ronnie.'

Detective Chief Inspector Glass helped himself to the rest of the champagne. 'A toast,' he smiled mischievously. 'To my forthcoming grandson, Jesus Basil Knox.'

THE END

We do hope that you have enjoyed reading this large print book.

Did you know that all of our titles are available for purchase?

We publish a wide range of high quality large print books including:
Romances, Mysteries, Classics
General Fiction
Non Fiction and Westerns

Special interest titles available in large print are:
The Little Oxford Dictionary
Music Book
Song Book
Hymn Book
Service Book

Also available from us courtesy of Oxford University Press:
Young Readers' Dictionary
(large print edition)
Young Readers' Thesaurus
(large print edition)

For further information or a free brochure, please contact us at:
Ulverscroft Large Print Books Ltd.,
The Green, Bradgate Road, Anstey,
Leicester, LE7 7FU, England.
Tel: (00 44) 0116 236 4325
Fax: (00 44) 0116 234 0205

BIRD

Jane Adams

Marcie has come to the bedside of her dying grandfather to make her peace. For Jack Whitney was the man who raised her, who loved her as if she was his own daughter, and from whom she ran away when she was just sixteen . . . But Jack is haunted by the terrible vision of a body hanging from a tree and the ghostly image of 'Rebekkah', a woman he insists is standing beside him, a noose around her neck. Marcie vows to uncover the true story behind this woman — even if it points to her grandfather being a murderer . . .

LAND OF MY DREAMS

Kate North

Maisie, an elderly lady, has lived in the shadow of her domineering and reclusive mother. Now her mother is dead and Maisie finally has a chance at life — one she comes to see and to experience through her new neighbours, the recently bereaved Clare and her teenage son, Joe. The unlikeliest of friendships begins as Joe, acting almost instinctively, draws Maisie out of her shell. Gradually, the secret that kept Maisie and her mother on the move and away from society is revealed, and Maisie finds the strength to make one last bid for happiness.